Emerald Coast

Finding her

By
TL KATT

Finding her Dragon

Emerald Coast

This book is a work of fiction. Any characters or events are purely figments of the author's imagination.

Published by Books by Elle, Inc.
225 College Dr. #65504
Orange Park, FL 32065
www.elleklass.weebly.com

Prologue

*J*att kept his mind focused on the task of escaping the vicious carnivores. The frigid air rushed over his body and wing tips. A burst of flames nipped at his feet as they moved in on him. He soared through the air, weaving, attempting to lose the ruthless beasts. He could not die but he could be injured.

The Fira were the most ruthless of all beasts on the planet. When the bright blue star burned out it left the planet, Preavym, a barren ice land. Many organisms went extinct. His kind, the Zaras, moved underground, salvaging any plant they could and building a garden, using artificial light. The ship his ancestors started was finished and would take them far away to a new home.

He swept across the dark sky, leading his followers away from the tunnels where his kind lived. His senses acute, the scent of ground Fira caught his nose. On the other side of the ridge.

They were close. If he could make it a little further, the Fira would kill and eat each other. Their lives were ones of pure survival, even if it meant devouring their own. He leaned and veered toward the icy range when fire reached from under him and eddied over his wings, burning them to a crisp. Unable to keep afloat, he crashed and slid across the icy surface, coming to rest against a frozen rock.

Within moments he was surrounded by flying Fira. His wings were worthless and blood oozed from his wounds, freezing almost on contact. He'd need blood to be whole again. As the Fira closed in he was ready with his razor-sharp teeth and claws. The Fira, unlike him, were not immortal. They could die. The Fira knew the strength and speed of the Zaras and how sharp their claws and teeth were but they didn't know that they were immortal.

They cautiously closed in on Jatt and were ready to fight, strings of flesh stuck between their bared teeth. The odor of death surrounding them.

Thick fur covered their bodies. Leathery wings on their backs. Jatt stepped forward as the Fira moved closer, circling him. There was a tunnel not far. If he killed one of the flying Fira the ground Fira would be on top of them in moments, giving him enough time to escape without being noticed.

With his heightened senses he heard the ground Fira. Their paws beat against the frozen ground, echoing in his ears. They smelled his blood. The Fira had a heightened sense of smell to find their prey but their hearing wasn't as developed as the Zaras. He swallowed, his eyes shifting from one Fira to the next. Without hesitation he sunk his teeth into the closest Fira and, with his razor claws, clipped the wings off it. Without waiting for the cannibalistic feast to begin he slipped away, while spitting out chunks of fur.

The sound of gnawing and screaming filled his ears as he moved towards the tunnel. Once inside, he had no time to rest. The ancestors shared

the stories of a time when
the planet flourished, and
all species lived
harmoniously together.
He had never known life
then. He was in the last
generation born and one
of the immortals. A group
developed in a lab to
outlive the planet and
take their species away
from it. To a new planet,
a new home where they
could once again live in
peace. They genetically
engineered them to be the
perfect species – flawless.
As a side effect they were
barren, and it was
impossible to grow the
population. It was

assumed that one day
they would overcome this
obstacle with science.

When the star had
given out and the plants
died the Fira began
eating. He couldn't stand
the thought of being
stuck on this planet
forever, alone with the
Fira for an eternity. The
planet he knew was only
bright the time of year it
circled the small, burning
star. When they swung
around the dead star
daylight was dim. His
kind had become
accustomed to the
underground, to darkness.
They only came out at

night to hunt. Their senses were keen. They didn't need light to see and could hear sounds for miles. They communicated silently with each other.

He pressed his hand against the wall. It opened. Dabina stood in wait.

"You don't look so good," she said, sweeping the hair from her forehead. "We'll get you fixed up." She stole a glance at his back.

Jatt scoffed, "Damn Fira." He didn't feel any more words were necessary.

Emerald Coast

They walked together and boarded the vessel. It was large enough for their entire population, including the various species of plants they managed to save. Jatt glanced back, taking one last glimpse at the only home he'd known as the steps swung upward, closing flush against the vessel. Once out of the planet's orbit the ship hit light speed.

They passed many solar systems, but none that possessed the potential for life that their planet once had. Then they came across a solar system of nine planets orbiting a single yellow star. The five planets orbiting furthest from the star were gas and ice and not suitable for life but the four planets closest to the star were small and solid. One of the planets, the third from the star, contained life already. It also had a moon, plentiful oxygen, and water.

They first sent out a team, as always when exploring a bioplanet. The team discovered it to be covered in plants and water. The atmosphere was thick and full of breathable oxygen. The planet contained a variety of life forms. Large, colorful animals dominated the land and their cousins dominated the seas and air. The moon gave off glowing light at night and the sun gave off a dynamic amount of light during the day. The Zaras determined this to be a good home and so they stayed. They landed their ship and buried it in what humans call Antarctica.

There were few humanoid creatures on the planet at the time. Dinosaurs covered the land, sea, and air. Smaller insects, amphibians, reptiles, and an assortment of microbial life existed. They were there and watched as the dinosaurs became extinct and were taken over by mammals. Later, humans, fully evolved, took over the Earth. To humans the Zaras were gods or demons. Many ancient civilizations learned from them. It was centuries into the existence of humans that the Fira and their-fire breathing cousins showed up.

Today, the Zaras are known as Vampires. The Fira, who morph, are

Emerald Coast

commonly called
werewolves or sometimes
'shape-shifter' but they
are one and the same.
Some are only able to take
the form of a single
animal but others can take
the shape of any. The
flying Fira, now extinct,
were dragons.

Chapter One

The high tide rolled in over the white sands as Abby sat on her third story balcony typing away on her laptop. Her fingers sweeping over the keys, she paused when a sound drifted to her ears. She glanced between the bars of the balcony and watched a young couple taking a late-night stroll along the beach. Their hands entwined and their gait slow as they meandered. She let out a sigh.

At nearly twenty-eight, she had no prospects. Most of her time was spent writing her latest bestseller. At twelve she entered her first story – a short story – into a writing contest with urging from her parents. She won the contest and her story was published. Her written language captivated many and she'd been publishing ever since.

At heart, she was a romantic who dreamed of finding her one true love.

If he existed. She was beginning to think he didn't. In her stories, the characters destined for one another found each other – their mushima – and mated for life.

As the case when writing a new story, she became the characters. Her mind seeing and hearing their every move and thought, seeping into her dreams. In her waking hours, the writing frenzy encompassed her and often she'd forget to eat and end up with a bowl of cereal when her stomach finally complained loud enough.

Emerald Coast

Her gaze leaving the young couple and shifting to the water, the gulf not as vast as the ocean, but water as far as the eye can see. It is the white sands that drew her to the gulf, much like the white sands in her story and she can see the small creatures playing in and out of the water, leaping on fish and playing with their food. She has a burning desire to join them. In her mind, she has lived many places in the world. Every place has special meaning to the book she is writing.

She focused once again on her story but

couldn't help feeling like she was being watched. This paranoia often happens when she writes. Letting out a deep breath, Abby stood, her hands resting against the metal balcony railing. The gulf breeze sweeping over her, pushing her hair over her shoulders. Her mind a trillion miles away, she jumped backwards when the doorbell rang.

Oh shit! Julian! She completely forgot. Julian was her best friend. She was lucky to have him. He took care of her. As a graphic artist he understood the *frenzy* but also found a way to compartmentalize work and play. She didn't have that balance.

She looked horrible in her cut-off purple sweat shorts and white tank top with no bra underneath. He was 100% happily gay and not concerned about her nips poking through, but he'd be disappointed in her general care. Her chestnut hair no doubt stuck out in odd angles as she'd rolled it into a messy bun. He would give her the speech. She braced for his words, his critical but true words as she opened the door.

His bright pink hair was pulled back in a short ponytail and, as always, he was dressed fashionably in a pair of blue Chino shorts with a grey-collared shirt and Birkenstock sandals. It was only practical when living near the beach to wear shoes that slipped on and off easily to dump sand. His eyes narrowed and brows formed a V while his blue pupils drifted over her frumpy appearance.

The aroma of the Chinese food drifted from the bag in his hand,

making her stomach
growl. He entered,
dropped the bag on the
table and said in animated
fashion, "Body, mind, and
spirit. Your chakras are all
off!" It wasn't that he was
completely into that stuff
but was open-minded to
almost anything.

Abby shrugged and
offered him a sheepish
smile while she opened
one of the bags and
reached in for a container
of food.

He placed his hand
over hers. "No, no, no.
Have you even showered?
You're not touching until

you take one," his voice forceful.

It was worthless to argue with him, so she dropped her hand. "I started a new book," she pleaded, even though she knew it would do no good.

"Abbs, I love you, but you have to love yourself and work on separating work from life."

He had alarms on his phone for everything. Time to spend working, at the gym, sleeping, having fun. He urged her regularly to make a schedule. Mostly this was because he worried about her wellbeing and checked on her regularly as he knew she had a difficult time separating work from everything else.

"Fine. I'm getting in the shower." She gave in, her stomach arguing with her decision.

After her shower she slipped on a fresh, clean pair of pink shorts and a white T-shirt with a flowery pink skull and cross bones on the front, then brushed her wet hair and marched into her dining/living room. Her condo had three rooms:

one bedroom, one bath, and the big room that was everything else. She spent most of her time on the balcony with the screen door wide open.

Julian used her time in the shower to spread the food on the table. She took a seat across from him and opened the Sichuan-style cucumber salad he'd brought for her. She was a vegetarian, while he on the other hand was completely omnivore, enjoying Orange chicken.

"Better," he smirked. "You're almost

presentable, but I guess it'll do."

She rolled her eyes as she shoved the first bite of the salad into her mouth. The plan was to head over to the Pirates Cove, a local beach bar, and have a few too many Zombies.

"Tell me about this new story," Julian said as he placed their first round of Zombies on the table.

They sat on the open-air deck as always. The soothing sounds of the tide louder tonight than usual and the gentle breeze carried conversations from every direction.

"You know… Maybe not. This one is kind of different. It's like a prequel maybe." The world her mind created was known as the Surrender Time Saga. All the past stories she'd written took place on Earth and were a mix of Gods and monsters, explaining everything from the building of the pyramids to the disappearance of Atlantis.

His face took on a concerned expression as

his lips pursed tightly together. "I have a meeting with my agent Friday. Why don't you come over Thursday for lunch and sangrias?"

It was their regular date to the Pirate's Cove every Tuesday that gave any structure of time and days of the week. "Sure. New book?" she asked. That was usually the reason he traveled to visit with his agent. He was a popular graphic artist.

"Something like that," he smiled.

After several Zombies between them, they stumbled back to her condo and passed out on the couch. Her mind drifting into the fictional world, envisioning the scene again. Jatt, with speed faster than any human eye could see but slow motion in her dream, slicing the wings off the Fira, escaping into the tunnel.

The Fira, bloody and damaged, his wings gone forever, lay against the cold ground. His chest barely moving. A lone ground Fira watches from a distance and, with a piece of humanity unknown yet to the Fira, feels remorse for the fire breathers, especially the one who has not only lost his wings but has been fed on as well. There aren't many places to hide, but the lone Fira knows of a cave not far away. She approaches the fire breather even though she knows helping him could be the death of her and she takes his near-lifeless body to the cave.

Deep into a mountain, the entrance not easy to find. She had been quietly tailing a Zaras when she had found it. She believed that somehow it was a Zaras tunnel but, after exploring the tunnel, she came up with only dead ends. She cared for the fire breathers. She couldn't explain why, emotions such as these were not a part of her Fira genetic imprint. The wingless fire breather had no life outside the tunnel, for he would die should he ever be found.

She hunted and brought back food for him, careful to never be tailed. She was especially fond of the fire breather who bore the scar of a Zaras bite. Waves of unexplained emotion and desire overtook her and she fell in love with the fire breather. He was incapable of the complexity of such an emotion but he did form a bond with her and she became pregnant. As two different closely-related species a pregnancy should have been impossible, yet it wasn't. Their offspring was neither fire breather nor Fira but a combination of the two. An abomination by all Fira standards but he was hers, theirs; a representation of them.

The offspring was able to shape-shift but only into fire breathing form and his wings were translucent, uncommon amongst Fira but not impossible. He was also able to breathe fire. She taught him to hunt as a fire breather but to never let another Fira see him in his other form. The fire breather she saved eventually died as all Fira, fire breather or ground, do. She continued to live and so did her offspring. He was beautiful in his regular form and, like her, had retractable teeth and claws; a feature she had never shown to other Fira.

Emerald Coast

It was her offspring
that discovered the secret
passageway in the hidden
tunnel where they resided.
Together they explored
the tunnel and learned
much about how the
Zaras lived. They
discovered the platform
from where the Zaras
ship had been built and
understood without direct
knowledge how it had
been built. They took this
discovery to the Fira, her
to the ground and him to
the fire breathers. They
were unique amongst
their kind and this was
insurance for their safety
should their secret ever be

discovered. Knowledge and discovery of anything Zaras was sacred amongst the Fira and against their primal code to destroy.

She and the offspring communicated on a level unknown to the Fira. They could read each other's minds and talk telepathically no matter how much distance was between them…

As the sun shone through the sliding glass door, Abby opened her eyes and looked around. She had fallen asleep on her couch again and had another crazy dream. The scent of green tea tickled her nose and she lifted an eyelid and watched Julian whip a bowl of egg substitute.

She strolled over to the balcony and enjoyed the sounds of the water rushing in and out. It brought about a feeling she thought of as home. The rising sun spread over the water. The gentle waves shimmering as they rolled over the white sands.

Chapter Two

fter a light breakfast of scrambled egg substitute and bread with jelly and green tea on the balcony, Julian left. Abby was alone with her thoughts and characters. Her mind anxious to spill the latest dream. She opened the file on the computer and went to work. A part of her mind was distracted by the gulf, the sands, and a sparkle

that kept catching her peripheral vision. She packed up her computer for the day and dressed in a simple lavender bikini. Tossing a see-through cover over her suit, she slipped on her favorite white flip flops and tossed a beach towel over her shoulder.

She told herself she was taking Julian's advice and spending quality time on a pleasure activity. One last glance from her balcony. The sparkle caught her eye again, but straight on as it sank beneath the water. A surfboard bobbed above it and a hand came up over the edge. A man lifted himself out of the water.

She couldn't move her eyes from him. He was perfect in every way physically possible. Long, dark, wet hair in a ponytail fell over his back. His body held a deep tan. Water glistened on his muscled shoulders as he swam on top of the board towards the shore. He was the epitome of utopia.

On the beach she spread out her towel and plunged her large umbrella into the sand. A

Emerald Coast

light wind kept the beach temperature from getting absurdly hot. It didn't take her roving eye long to find the man on his surfboard. The Emerald Coast wasn't known for surfing. The waters were quite shallow and not rough enough to form large waves, but it didn't seem to bother him.

Hidden by dark sunglasses, she kept her eye on him while she listened to her favorite playlist on her phone. She imagined the two of them in a steamy love scene, hot sex where he pounded her on the beach, the tide rushing over them and then receding. In her mind there was no one else on the beach but the two of them.

After hours of surfing he came onto the beach, his board tucked under his arm. He walked straight towards her with a look so intense she almost had to look away. He was even more beautiful up close. *Was he aware she'd been watching him? Daydreaming?* She suddenly felt nervous and awkward.

He undid his ponytail; his hair fell,

hanging just below his shoulders. It was the color of dark-roasted coffee and his eyes were so radiant. She felt as though she could see inside his soul. His heart pounded in his chest, a steady rhythm in her ears. For a moment she felt as though their minds connected. *That's impossible, Abby. Pull your eyes away,* she thought as he grew closer, only a few feet from her now.

In that instant the world stood still and a primordial urge from somewhere deep within her welled to the surface.

It was a feeling she had never felt before but it guided her actions as he dropped onto the sand beside her.

He gave her a quick smile as he grabbed a towel and threw it over his shoulders and picked up a pair of flip flops. *How stupid can you be?! He wasn't interested in you. You planted yourself by his stuff!* The awkward feeling returned as she felt like an idiot. Shifting her eyes from him, she acted nonchalant.

At home she slapped together an avocado, garlic sandwich on rye

and turned on the TV.
Pouring a glass of
Chardonnay, she spent
the evening streaming her
favorite shows and
playing catch up. The
man stayed in her mind.
His glistening body, water
rolling down his chest and
back.

His lips pressed
against hers, his finger
tracing the small of her
back. She leaned her head
back as he kissed her
neck, then her chest. His
fingers moving beneath
her panties, finding her
sweet spot. Moans
escaped her lips as she
met his passion with her

own, fondling his manhood, stroking it gently in her fist. Her lips and tongue exploring his body.

The two were linked together on her living room floor, with the sound of the surf and the cool night breeze coming through the opened sliding glass door. Abby let out a gasp and moan with her orgasm, feeling his warmth inside her. His hot, heavy breath against her neck. He'd cum too.

She couldn't remember the events that had brought them to that moment to her living

room floor. She could
only remember a
consuming desire and an
impassioned pleasure. It
was like nothing in life
she had ever experienced.
The two lay naked on the
floor, embracing, not a
word said between them,
and they fell asleep.

In her dreams she
did not dream of the Fira
but of the Zaras, the
Vampires. A female who
was lonely and felt
nothing but despair;
immortality was more of a
curse than an
evolutionary blessing. She
had lived for so long that
she had lost track of time

and wanted nothing more than a child of her own. Yes, they had discovered how to impregnate human women with Vampire sperm but why were female Vampires cursed and unable to carry a fetus?

Maybe the problem was human men. No Vampire had ever considered a shape-shifter as a viable option, as they were considered vile, savage beasts. With a single burning desire for a child, she searched for a shape-shifter that did not repulse her. She found one and he was beautiful and different. Not only could she listen to his thoughts, but she went deep inside his cells, into the heart of the nucleus and read the story of his DNA.

He was not full shape-shifter, as she knew by looking at him, but was more than half. His father had been a full shifter, but his mother was only half, the other half human. In her desperation, she seduced him. It had been easy, as Vampires were as beguiling to shape-shifters as they were to humans. She kept a sample of his semen and drank some of his blood so she would forever be able to find him. He would never remember the experience, but she would have a child, his child.

After many trials, she conceived. No Vampire had conceived since the immortal generation had been born. She had a beautiful son with endless dark eyes. They contained the secret of both species – a lethal, hybrid combination. His transparent wings could only be seen as a shimmer across his back. He looked more Vampire

than shape-shifter. She
had hoped he would stay
that way but when he
reached puberty he
shifted for the first time.
First, into a jaguar.

She didn't know if he
subconsciously chose
what to shift into or if it
was programmed, but he
had always loved jaguars.
He spent his childhood in
South America and had
spent hours admiring
them as a child. When he
shifted for the first-time,
she found him running
and playing with other
jaguars. She learned to
appreciate this quality in
him and at times felt

jealous, as she could not join him in his hunt as a jaguar, only in his hunt as a Vampire.

As he reached adulthood, she found his shifting quality was not limited to jaguars but he could become a tiger shark as well. Now tiger sharks aren't picky about their food and, when he shifted into one, neither was he. It was his most ancient of instincts that drove the shift and he was ruthless on the hunt as a shark. This quality she didn't desire, it was the Fira genes within him. They had been the most

vicious of hunters. She
loved her child none the
less. He had grown up in
her Vampire world but
was not an immortal yet.
He enjoyed human blood
and the blood of many
other mammals, but soon
he would have to drink
Vampire blood, her
blood, to truly be
immortal.

Abby arose with the
sun streaming across her
naked body. The beautiful
man was gone but maybe
he had never been there
and he was some sort of
dream. All the doors and
windows were locked,
except the sliding glass

door leading to the balcony, so unless he could fly or jump three stories without breaking a bone he had been nothing more than an illusion.

She leaned backwards onto the floor and ran her palms over her cheeks and hair. *I imagined that. It felt so real. It's been way too long, Abbs.*

Chapter Three

With a steaming cup of green tea, Abby took to her balcony and opened her computer. Her mind not completely focused on her work. It wandered to the beach, the gulf, the chance of seeing him again. All she could think of was seeing him again, indulging in his glory. He was like a drug and she was addicted after one solitary, amazing evening that probably was a dream. One eye on the water, waiting to catch another glimpse of him.

After a few unsuccessful hours of unimpressive work, she walked to the local dive bar – The Shell. It was a small hut on the beach. The bar wrapped around the center where a single bartender worked his magic. The wind in her hair, the foamy water washing over the sand.

After several drinks, she took a leisurely stroll along the beach. Her feet in the water, she dropped onto the sand and lay backwards, her eyes closed. Water rushed under her legs, butt, and back as she imagined the dark-eyed god of a man. Within moments she was above the water, gliding gracefully, racing a shark, the shark so quick and agile in the water, his skin shimmering beneath the water's surface.

Then she was with him again, wrapped in his arms, their bodies entwined on the beach, rolling in the sand. It was as she had imagined the previous day.

She awoke in the morning, neatly tucked

into her bed, unable to recall how she got home. The last thing she remembered was dropping onto the sand and the dream. A quiet thumping made her jump. She realized it was her dryer. She slipped her silk robe sloppily over her shoulders and pulled the drawer next to her bed open, careful not to make any noise. Grasping the heavy flashlight she kept as a just-in-case-I-need-it weapon, she tiptoed into the big room. *Thump, thump.*

She grasped the closet door. Holding the

flashlight above her in case she needed to come down hard on someone or something she turned the knob, revealing her washer and dryer. She glanced to her front door, which was locked, the patio wide open, but she was on the third floor. It was highly unlikely anyone would come or go from there. That was one of the reasons she chose a condo on the third floor.

The floor was free of sand. It was never sand-free. Rushing into the bathroom, her bikini was hanging from the side of the tub. There was no sand in the tub or on the floor. Perplexed, she sat on the edge of her bed. *Is he real?* It was the only explanation, even though she knew it was impossible.

Abby had choices: to dwell on her vivid imagination that was seeping into the real world or write. If she chose to dwell on her vivid imagination, then she'd have to accept she was losing her marbles. She didn't approve of that option.

Clouds rolled in from the ocean, bringing rain and a cooler than usual breeze. Instead of working on the patio she took to her couch, pulled a microfiber lavender blanket over her legs and got to work.

The Zaras who had escaped the fire breathing Fira before exiting the planet was a lead fertility scientist on Earth, his most recent Earth name was Jim. He had chosen the name because of its meaning, someone who uses trickery. He had helped make hybrid Vampires. He had never used his DNA but that of donor Vampires. All hybrids were kept in a data base and only a specific number were allowed to be made.

Since they, too, were immortal, the Earth could not be over-populated with beings that lived forever. The world would become a very crowded place if everyone born was immortal. There had to be a balance between those that died and the very top of the food chain, those that never did.

He had grown to admire the simplicity of the human life. In the past, as generations died, many ideas died with them, but with the humans' increases in technology information lived on and was kept as a record, much like the Vampire mind. Still, they were human and no matter how great a human, eventually, they died.

Time for Jim stood still. Humans wanted so much what Vampires had, eternal life and youth. He didn't want his youth or eternal life anymore. He wanted what humans had, death. He fell in love with a beautiful human named Rose. He knew her life would be but a speck compared to his. He wanted her still. She was beautiful to him and perfect.

He married her and they had a child, a gorgeous little girl. He knew Rose wanted a baby girl and so he gave his Rose what she wanted. He was a geneticist and meticulously designed their daughter. She would show no Vampire characteristics until she was a grown woman. At that time, she could make a decision as to whether she would choose an immortal Vampire life or that of a human.

Emerald Coast

He had left his home planet while he was still young and they had taken Earth as a second home. It was much like the stories of their ancestors that were imprinted in their brains. What would happen when Earth's star died? They would gather, exhume the ship, and leave again for a destination unknown. He did not want to leave, nor did he want to live without his Rose. No creature should live forever.

He envisioned that his ancestors had programmed his

generation to be immortal, but if life could be given it could also be taken. He spent his time apart from his family searching for answers to kill the unkillable. As much as he didn't want a life without Rose, he didn't want his daughter to suffer his fate of eternity should she chose immortality. Forever was a very long time.

Rose always knew Jim was something more than human. He didn't go out during the day unless it was overcast. Instead of a beach honeymoon, she settled for a cabin on a

secluded lake. He was
more intelligent than any
man she had ever met and
never aged. It was as if
the fountain of youth
existed inside him. She
had many holes in her
memory.

It was when their
daughter, Sabia, was
thirteen that he finally
confided the truth to
Rose. She was shocked at
first. Her lips opened but
no words came out for
several minutes. Finally,
she said: "No. Vampires
don't exist. That's silly.
They're legends designed
by simple people who
couldn't explain the

strange things they witnessed. Are you okay? Should I take your temperature?"

Her thinking and concern tickled him and his lips curled into a smile. "No. I'm healthy, Rose."

He took her hands in his and closed his eyes. The gaps in her memory became filled as his thoughts and memories streamed into her mind. Her eyes widened with each one. How could she be married to him all these years and never know such a big secret. A part of her melted. *Why didn't he trust her before?* She accepted that everything he did was for their family. Such a large secret could possibly put their lives in danger.

She stood and tugged at his shirt, pulling it upwards. She ran her fingers across his bare back. Her eyes fully open to what he was, she ran her fingers over his wings. They were beautiful, shimmering in the light. A rainbow of colors. She swallowed before spitting out her next words. "I'm sure you had good reason for not sharing this, but we're a team. I feel let down. You can always trust me." Her eyes grew watery.

He nodded. "I know, love. I should have said something sooner. I'm still Jim. Please forgive me," he begged. The sadness and fear in her eyes overwhelmed him.

She nodded. Yes, she forgave him, but still felt saddened by his actions. Their daughter. Panic seized her. *Was she human or Vampire?* She feared the answer but had to know the truth. "Our daughter?"

"She is human and can choose a human life

or a Vampire life. The choice will be hers when she is an adult and old enough to make the decision. If she chooses a Vampire life she will also become immortal." It was bad enough telling her their precious daughter would have the choice to become a Vampire, telling her she'd become immortal if she chose that life was even more difficult. He broke the most innate of Vampire code, telling a human.

Rose knew one day she would die. Should their daughter choose immortality she would

not. As the final nail in
the coffin, Jim disclosed
that he was searching for
a way to end his life. He
wanted to die with her
but she couldn't accept
that, their daughter
roaming the Earth and
universe with no mother
or father. She begged him
to stay immortal or to
make her immortal too so
they would always have
each other. Jim refused
and said it was impossible
to make her like him: 'I
was born the way I am
and would not wish what
I am on any human,
especially not my Rose.'

Emerald Coast

Feeling a sense of accomplishment, Abby put her computer away and meandered onto the balcony. Resting her hands on the railing, she watched the tide roll in and out as the sun lowered itself on the horizon.

After a couple hours of TV she got up and stared at the open sliding glass door. She rarely closed it, but considered maybe she should. For two nights the dream man had come to her, left physical evidence that someone was in her house; clothes in the washing machine that she hadn't put there, every spot of sand swept. It gave her stomach an eerie feeling.

This was a test. If he was real, he wouldn't come see her if the door was closed. If it was her imagination and lack of a sex life, then he would still come to her. Abby gripped the handle and slid the door, then turned it to the lock position, bolted the top and searched her house for something long and thick to put in the bottom track. She found a long, thick piece of wood left

over from when her
father installed shelves in
her bedroom to house her
collection of books.

Dropping that into
the track, there wasn't
much give and should
keep out any horny,
good-looking young man.
She then locked and dead
bolted the front door as
well as sliding the chain.
Satisfied, she went to bed
and, as an added measure,
locked the bedroom door
and the door connecting
the bedroom to the
bathroom. Her condo a
one bedroom, one bath.
The bathroom opened

into her room and the
entryway.

Chapter Four

The sun streamed across Abby, begging her to wake up. She stretched and slowly opened her eyes. The man hadn't come. Her dreams weren't filled with hot sex and orgasms, but her characters.

In a long T-shirt with no underwear beneath, green tea in hand, she checked her door locks. All were in place. *He's real?* Her mind debated.

She sighed, set down her green tea and opened the sliding glass door. The room felt so stuffy, probably because she had forgotten to turn on the air. The fresh ocean breezes made air conditioning nonessential.

She got to work as she sipped at her tea.

The ground Fira and her half-breed offspring, Xenos, boarded the ship with all the other Fira. There were two ships: the ground took one, and the fire breathers the other. She hated to not be with her son but he was a fire breather in their eyes.

Emerald Coast

They did not know the truth. On their journey, they ravaged many planets. There were few in the universe stronger than them.

There'd been one other planet with a species powerful enough to harm them. It was a beautiful planet, green with plants. The waters a shimmering teal. It reminded her so much of Preavym, but the inhabitants with their pointy ears and sharp features weren't pushovers. They drove the Fira back to the ship and off their planet.

She killed to squelch her hunger, not for fun. Fira had no conscience and killed for pleasure as much as they did for hunger. Xenos also had a conscience, a soul.

Xenos, like his mother, did not completely understand the way of the Fira. He had always had trouble excepting that he was one of them: a vile, indignant creature. They liked nothing more than to ravage life. He loved life. As much as he enjoyed tearing the pulsing flesh from a body he, enjoyed the blood; sweet, delectable, succulent blood. It contained oxygen which was intoxicating to him. It was a life force that made him stronger. He could enchant other Fira.

More than anything, Xenos hoped their new home would allow him the opportunity to be not only a flying fire breather, but be a place he could stretch out his claws and teeth; a home where he could be himself.

On Earth, he found that home. He didn't live as a dragon but as his other self, the one he had always hidden. The Earth had inhabitants: humans. Humans were more depraved and disgusting than Fira. They were savages but not as strong as the pointed-eared savages they'd encountered in their travels. Nevertheless, humans drove all flying Fira to extinction.

He was all that was left of them. As the generations passed, no one but he and his mother knew. He still enjoyed flying but, unlike his moronic cousins, he displayed his dragon self in only the most remote areas. He enjoyed humans

and blended in beside
them. They could not see
what those of his kind
could and he found they
were enchanted with him
much like the Fira.

Humans were not
alone; all around them,
unbeknownst to them,
were Vampires. They saw
Vampires as like
themselves because they
couldn't see with their
human eyes what he
could see. His senses and
vision were much sharper
than those of humans.
Vampires radiated a
shimmering glow; the
same shimmering glow
that enveloped him after

drinking the blood of a beast. He wanted to meet another like him. He was neither Fira, nor human, nor Vampire. *What was he?*

It was after centuries that he found her. She was neither human nor Vampire but a combination of the two. She had skin softer than the finest silk and her eyes were emeralds set against the glow of her skin. They could speak through their minds. She did not yet know her Vampire heritage and did not yet seek the life force of blood. She desired him as much as he desired her.

Emerald Coast

Honk, Honk, Honk, Honk… The annoying alarm on Abby's phone blared at her. She chose the most annoying sound so it would force her to get going or wake up. Stopping the horrible honking, she saved her work, logged out of the computer, and stretched before standing.

The alarm was her reminder that today she was visiting Julian before his visit to his publisher. The trips usually only lasted a few days but, in that time, she'd miss him. It was because of him and his insisting on scheduling activities that she'd set the alarm.

Julian lived shoreside. He didn't like the idea of being stuck on a large sandbar during a hurricane. But the large sandbar was perfect for her. It was like its own little town. They had a small strip of condos no more than three stories high, as city ordinances didn't allow a taller structure. They had the Pirate's Cove, The Shell, and a food truck at the beach daily with chicken strips, corndogs, French fries, hamburgers, and other junky snack foods and drinks. One gas station that doubled as a corner grocery, pharmacy, and post office.

She rarely left the large sandbar, as Julian dubbed it. Nirvana Isle was its proper name and it was part of the greater Nirvana Inlet area. A small town in Florida on the gulf coast, famously known as the Emerald Coast for its white sands and sparkling emerald water.

Dressed in an airy yellow blouse and denim shorts she threw her purse over her shoulder when her phone buzzed in her back pocket. Julian. *Get off the computer,* was his loving message.

She texted back. *Way ahead of you.*

He replied with a laughing face emoji.

Julian's house was over the short bridge, not too far inland. Abby pulled her car into his driveway. Hibiscus surrounded his house and bougainvillea wound up a trellis by his front door showing off its showy pink leaves. Its sweet scent filling her nostrils, mixed with peanuts, spinach, pineapple, and blueberries. *Impossible!*

There's no way I can smell all that.

The scents mingled in her nasal passages. She figured it was her stomach complaining since she hadn't eaten yet. Before she had a chance to ring the bell Julian opened the door. "I like. You look human."

She play-punched his arm as she entered. The Breakfast Club was streaming on his TV. He loved the 80s Brat Pack movies. "You ever watch anything else?"

"No," he said with a wink as he wrapped her in

his arms with a welcoming hug.

When they separated, she followed him into the kitchen. She stopped at the bar and took a seat while he moved around to the other side and poured red liquid with fruit chunks into a glass and slid it along the counter. "My own special Sangria."

The flavor burst in her mouth and coated her taste buds as she took the first drink. He grabbed a salad from the fridge and sprinkled slivered nuts on it as he passed it to her. "I made this up today. I call it a fru-veg. It's delicious, but the peanuts are to die for. Try it."

Julian's creativity didn't end with comic books and art. He had a myriad of talents from an eye for landscaping and interior decorating to cooking and prepping meals. His home had a masculine touch with the large black leather sectional, sixty-five inch LCD and surround sound. Modern, slim tables accented the living room area and a few tasteful pictures hung on the walls. His home was one of comfort and style.

She didn't hesitate in taking her first bite. She chewed and swallowed, flavor bursting in her mouth. "Wow! That is delicious! That might be the best one yet," she said before shoveling in another bite.

His lips curled into a smile as he took a seat beside her with some type of shrimp dish. Even though she was a vegetarian it made her mouth water. As the moments between them passed with light conversation her mind convinced her she needed to try a bite of his shrimp.

Emerald Coast

No, No, No! She convinced herself, staving off the urge to ask him for one.

"The pool temperature is eighty-five degrees. What do you say?" he asked, clearing their dishes.

She refilled their Sangrias. Most likely she had a suit there. Whenever she came over it became an all-nighter as among his gifts was mixology. The sun was bright above the pool. The screen that housed the patio and pool nothing to keep the sun's radiation away. It mostly kept out the bugs, leaves, and other larger creatures that could really mess up a pool in Florida.

Abby slipped on an old suit she had there and padded to the screen room. Julian already floating in the pool, his hands behind his head, waiting for her, a sangria placed in the floaties cupholder. She glimpsed the pan on the stove. Inside, a couple shrimp. She grabbed them and popped them into her mouth before she considered what she was doing. Her body didn't protest the delicious little crustaceans covered in a creamy garlic sauce.

She set her sangria on the edge and jumped in, making a big splash so as to spray water on Julian. When she brought her head above the water, his legs were soaked. She offered a silly smile.

"Really? You just did that?"

She crinkled her nose as she lifted herself onto a floatie. "I did." She paddled towards the side and grabbed her sangria.

The sweet scents of blooming flowers drifted up her nose. Lately, she'd felt her senses were overwhelmed, especially smell. Her taste buds, too. Flavors exploded in her mouth and then there was the little thing with the beautiful man from the beach. She'd locked the doors and he hadn't come. That justified in her mind that he was real.

Every part of her wanted to tell Julian. To spill the weird things happening to her. He wouldn't judge, yet a little voice inside told her not to. He'd remind her how important it was to keep a schedule and eat right. Bringing her mind to the shrimp. She had really eaten shrimp. "So what do you have going on with your agent?" she asked.

He set his sangria in the cup holder and swallowed. "Have you ever thought monsters might exist?"

"Like the boogeyman? No, he's not real, but witches maybe. They could be real."

"I'm thinking more like werewolves and Vampires."

She leaned back and tilted her head to glimpse his face. "Sure, absolutely. I write about them, you know."

"Okay, so think about this. They are real. Werewolves are nasty creatures who kill, but Vampires are something like Gods. Somehow in the mix, humans being prey and pawns they develop extrasensory skills such as precognition, telepathy, telekinesis, and witches are definitely real." His voice edged with a seriousness he usually saved for her terrible lifestyle. He meant business.

"Let's say that's true. How did humans get

these extrasensory skills?"
she asked.

"They evolved,
enhanced naturally." His
answer matter-of-fact.
"But Vampires and
werewolves don't know."

She leaned her head
backwards against the
float's pillow and stared
into the sky which
seemed brighter today
even through her
sunglasses. "Okay, I can
roll with that." Her stories
were about dragons,
werewolves, and
vampires, although they
weren't called those
names. It's still what they

are, but the human aspect wasn't part of her stories.

The water moved as he slowly paddled towards her. "Vander is a human who is a precog. He and other humans have these evolved skills. For their survival, they must keep them secret from the monsters. They have their own society in which they shield and govern each other. There are rules and a covenant to follow."

"I love it! This is your new idea?" It was like the human aspect of the world she'd created and she'd never considered the human side.

He caught her float with his foot. "Yup, that's why I'm seeing my agent. I've drawn out several roughs and have enough to present. I think he'll buy it."

"In today's world, hell yeah. People eat this stuff up. Look at my book sales. I hit the bestseller list as a child!" She paddled her float around, his foot dropping off the back and grabbed onto the side of his, pulling herself closer.

"When we get out, I'll show you what I have." He winked at her.

She loved his creativity and art and had a few signed copies in cases on her living room wall at home. "I love the human aspect. Why not have humans with super-powers like the X-men or something?"

"Except my characters fight true monsters not just other enhanced humans."

Chapter Five

Abby stayed in Julian's extra room after drinking far too many sangrias to safely drive anywhere. She kissed her friend good-bye as she left his home. Instead of going straight to her condo she decided today she had other things to do. Normal stuff she didn't usually do. Strange things were happening to her. She feared her imaginary world was seeping into reality, as Julian always suggested.

Her first stop: the grocery store. She wheeled her cart down the aisle, stock-piling her regular items when she was interrupted in thought. She felt as though somebody else was inside her brain, her thoughts jumped around inside her head without her permission.

As she passed the meat aisle, a sudden urge to buy meat consumed her. She had always been a vegetarian. Her parents were devout carnivores.

They hunted regularly and always had a supply of venison, wild turkey, and other animals in the freezer. They found her strange and gave each other knowing glances saying, "One day you will crave meat."

Was today the day? Is this what they meant? She'd eaten the shrimp yesterday. The odor of flesh and coppery scent of blood flooded her nostrils and overtook her body as she lifted a steak from the bin, bringing it closer to her nose. She wanted to stuff it all in her mouth raw. The thought terrified her as she suddenly dropped it.

Her mouth salivating, the urge rising again she picked it up and placed it in her cart. Abby's mind and urges arguing against each other, finally deciding she should at least try it.

At home she put up her groceries including the *meat*. She stared at the steak, not sure why she even bought it. The idea of eating it repulsed her and excited her at the same time. She considered calling her mother, but reconsidered. Today wasn't the day she wanted to hear about all the reasons she should eat meat.

Time to herself, that's what Julian preached, and that's what she'd do the rest of the day. No better way to relax and do for *her* than a massage and a facial.

The mixed herbal aromas blasted her nose when she opened the door to Nirvana Day Spa. Light blue velvet chairs were separated with floral arrangements and relaxation stones on tables between them.

"Can I help you?" asked Karen, according to

her name tag. Her short, blond hair in a bob and a smile on her face.

She knew she should have called and scheduled, but things in her life happened on whims. "Can I get a massage and even a facial for today?"

Karen swished her lips as she scanned the appointment book with her finger. "Yes, I can get you in for the facial now. Someone just cancelled and the massage…I can fit you in with Enrique after." She glanced up, her green eyes beaming.

Lucky, that was it. This place was always packed, but today the seats were nearly empty save for a young, dark-haired woman. "Perfect. Thank you."

"Simone will be out in a minute to assist you. Would you like a glass of wine while you wait?"

Wine, the snack of champions. Other than the light breakfast Julian cooked she hadn't eaten. "Yes, thank you."

She took a seat in the comfy chair. Her butt sinking into the soft material and puffy cushion. Within minutes, a middle-aged woman approached her with a glass of wine in hand.

"I'm Simone," she said, handing her the glass as she instructed Abby to follow her, change, and gave her a key to a locker.

Abby changed and, a few minutes later, Simone knocked on the door and led her to a room infused with aromatic scents that instantly relaxed her. Her mind slipped away as the woman applied the mask, and the soothing sounds of the tide lulled her mind. A slice of sheer heaven, she couldn't help feeling slight disappointment when it was over.

Enrique was a pleasant surprise and complete eye candy. Thick, dark, wavy hair, his skin naturally tan and brown eyes so dark they almost looked black. With his fine features he looked more like a super model than a masseuse. Her eyes drifted from his face to his arms and pecs as muscles exploded beneath his shirt.

His hands and arms worked magic as they pushed and kneaded on her muscles and tissues. She hadn't realized how tight and knotted she was until he loosened everything. Her arms, shoulders, top of her legs, and feet.

She turned over, her face in the donut and her body clay in Enrique's hands. Her mind emptied as every tense muscle loosened. A lush, green world filled the spaces of her cerebrum. Small creatures flitted carefree, soaking in the radiance of the giant star. Its heat bathed her soul.

She was no longer Abigail but a young Zaras from long, long ago before they built cities

and societies, buzzing
from flower to flower,
indulging in the succulent
nectar of each plant. Her
wings glowed with vibrant
sparkling lights that
communicated with the
others. She went high into
the flowering trees,
hidden by their glory.

Darkness replaced
the light of the dual stars
and coldness swept over
her heart, her body. A
sharp pain radiated
through her back and she
was suddenly back in the
spa, Enrique still moving
his enchanted fingers
across her back. The
pleasure she'd felt gone,

replaced with sharp waves of pain. She jumped off the table!

Enrique, flabbergasted, gawked at her with wide eyes as she wrapped the towel around her and rushed out of the room to the changing area with the locker.

A long, wide mirror hung on the wall. She tilted her shoulder forward and stared at her back in the mirror. It looked normal. Opening the locker, she threw out her clothes and rummaged through her purse until she found a pen.

Emerald Coast

She pressed it against
the area causing the pain,
not understanding what
was wrong. Confused, she
looked one more time at
her back and it twinkled
at her. Closing her eyes
and then reopening them,
she looked again, and the
twinkle was gone but her
skin appeared to glow. *I'm
going crazy or they drugged the
wine*, she thought,
knowing there were no
drugs in the wine. It was
probably the
consumption of wine on a
near-empty stomach.

Dressed, she paid her
bill, left a generous tip
and walked into the bright

afternoon light, shoving dark glasses over her eyes. A silvery-blue sedan crawled past Nirvana Massage, grabbing her attention. Its slow motion is what caught her. It was as if it was searching for an address. Dismissing it, she got into her car and started the engine when her phone rang. Abby glanced at the ID. Mom. She ignored it. She'd call her back once she got home.

Meridian Subs called to her as she spotted it at the light. They had the most delicious veggie wrap in all Nirvana. Her stomach grumbled at the thought, urging her to eat. She pulled into the parking lot and from the corner of her eye spotted the silvery-blue sedan. *Is it following me?* A shiver ran up her spine. Convincing herself it probably wasn't the same one, and even if it was it was silly to think they were following her.

She noted a couple eating close to the window. The man who looked like he ate out a lot with his round figure had a Philly Cheese on the plate in front of him. The strange meat urges roared inside her as her mind battled between ordering one or her normal veggie wrap.

The Philly Cheese winning the battle as she couldn't believe the words coming from her mouth. Had she really ordered that? Her logic told her to try meat before she went home and devoured the steak in her fridge.

Unwrapping the sub, she stared at it, then wrapped her hand around it and brought it to her mouth. The mixture of scents swirled through her nose as she sank her teeth into it. *Bliss, absolute bliss!* Bite after bite, her taste buds and entire body erupted in a stir of emotions she'd never known. This is what her parents had warned her about: 'One day you will desire meat.'

Her mind on a meat high, she stared out the window. A silvery-blue sedan pulling into the parking lot. Her eyes widened as she stuffed the last bite of the sandwich into her mouth and scurried out the door opposite from where they parked. She rushed to her car and jumped in and exited through the adjacent parking lot of the supermarket next door.

A voice in her head said, *They're coming for you.* A sense of urgency bolted through her veins as she pulled out of the parking lot and into the subdivision behind the shopping center. She knew all the back roads and would stay on them until she had to go over the bridge.

She kept an eye pealed for the silvery sedan, checking her rear view every few seconds but didn't see them again. To be on the safe side she entered the large garage

of her condo building
through the back entrance
for owners and tenants
only. She parked and
glanced out her window,
sure she was alone. She
exited her car and was
running to the elevator
when two men stepped
out from behind the wall.

One tall and
muscled, the other
shorter. Their eyes fixed
on her as she stopped
mid-stride and gulped.
Her heartbeat quickened
and time slowed. Bones
snapped and cracked as
their bodies morphed into
something else. Their
noses elongated and claws

erupted from their hands and feet.

Her brain didn't think as her body reacted. In a surreal moment, sharp claws extended from her hands and plunged directly into the chest cavities of both wolf men. She watched their bodies drop to the ground, blood spewing from open arteries, its warmth coating her flesh. The iron, coppery scent coaxed, teased her mind.

In a moment of lucidity, she felt their warm, lifeless hearts in her palms, blood streaming to her bent

Emerald Coast

elbows. She swallowed hard. The aroma of fresh blood took control and she dropped the hearts and lowered herself to the ground. Sharp teeth erupted from her gums as she sank them into one of the men and then the other, drinking in the fresh blood.

Chapter Six

bby woke up on her couch in the living room of her condo. *Had she dreamed the whole thing?* It seemed real. She still tasted the blood in her mouth, remembering their fleshy hearts in her hands. She brought her hands to her face. They weren't stained, there wasn't blood anywhere on them, her arms, or her clothes. Checking herself

in the bathroom, her clothes were bloodless.

Still not convinced that it didn't happen she sprinted to the parking garage. Her lungs unaffected. She should be breathing hard but wasn't. She went to the exact spot. There were no dead bodies, no abandoned hearts or anything. The cement floor appeared normal. She traced her steps to and from her car and every inch of the garage and elevator. Nothing!

Perplexed, she didn't know what to think. *Is it my imagination? A dream?* It felt so real, incredibly real. It couldn't have been a dream. Was she going crazy?

She sat cross legged on the garage floor and closed her eyes. A stream of consciousness, not her own, flowed through her brain, neuron to neuron. Dishes clanking, people eating dinner, children running and playing, TV sets blaring and the ocean, the calm serene sound of the tide. Her mind focused on the tide, the vast, endless ocean.

How was she hearing so much? It wasn't possible, was it? Convinced something was happening to her, she marched back to her condo. Her head in a tizzy. It was time to call Mom.

"Hi, baby," her mom said in her gentle voice. The TV in the background

"Hi, Mom," she answered, unsure how to start the conversation.

"Your twenty-eighth birthday is next week. Your dad and I will be there."

Great! She's having a mental breakdown and her mom is concerned about her birthday. "I'm really busy now with work. I started a new story and it's eating up all my time. Maybe we can postpone—"

"I won't hear of it. You can take one day off. Twenty-eight is a big deal. We're going to be there. That's that." Her voice forceful. Abby knew *the voice*. She had no choice, and even if she went on a cruise halfway across the world her parents would track her down. Her father had excellent stealth tracking skills. There was no escape.

Instead of arguing, Abby changed the subject. "Is there any

incidence of mental illness in the family?"

"Why do you ask such a silly question?"

"Just answer, Mom."

"Is there something wrong?" her voice beaming with concern.

Abby sighed heavily into the phone. She wanted a straight answer.

"No, baby. No mental illness on either side. You come from a family with impeccable health and genes."

"How did my grandparents die?"

She heard the confusion and concern in her mom's voice as she spoke. "Baby, they were all old. We've told you before. Why are you asking? Is there something going on that I should know about?"

Her mother's mother had died of old age and her grandfather a broken heart. The night she died, he lay beside her and gave up living. Abby was an infant and didn't remember ever meeting them. Her mother died of natural causes and father an accident when he was a young boy. His mother raised him, and died of natural causes at an old age. They were old

people, and old people
die.

"Nothing, Mom.
Listen, I have to go,
Julian's at the door," she
lied, wanting the
conversation to end.

"You give him a hug
for me. Love you, baby."

"I love you too,
Mom. I'll see you next
week."

That was it. Not the
answer she wanted.
Under other
circumstances she'd be
happy, but something was
happening to her.
Something she had no
explanation for and
learning that Grandpa

was schizophrenic would give her a starting point, something tangible to know which direction to go.

Her emotions swarmed and all she wanted was her mom's arms wrapped tight around her as she cried into her shoulder. A tear ran down her cheek. She swiped it away and sniffled. Crying wouldn't help her figure this out, but it would release all the anxiety. The tears flowed free and she didn't stop them as she pressed her head into one of the throw pillows on the couch until she fell asleep.

She awoke to a room coated in the golden and pink rays of the sunset. Her stomach a grumbling mess. She didn't have time to take food out and prepare a meal so she pushed on her sunglasses and left her condo. The walk might do her good. The fresh air and exercise.

Barefoot, the wet sand squished between her toes. She liked the feeling. She approached The Shell, which was open. They were always open unless a hurricane was brewing offshore. A couple of older gentlemen sat at the bar, discussing the stock market. She guessed they spent their mornings as retired folk day trading. The conversation wasn't too interesting to her.

"Here you go," the bartender, a middle-aged woman with double E boobs and dark hair, said as she handed her the drink. Jilly wasn't the only bartender, but usually worked evenings when Abby went out.

"Thanks," Abby said as she lifted the drink to her lips. The mojito went down smoothly. Her taste buds capturing the lime, sugar, and mint. The flavors burst in her mouth.

Her feet squished in the sand as she walked to the food truck. The line wasn't long and her loaded cheese fries didn't take long either. She carried them and the bottled water she ordered to a small area with benches. Palm trees, swaying in the wind, surrounding her.

A woman in a large floppy hat strolled to the little area and towards the table where Abby sat.

"Do you mind?" the woman asked. Her voice carried an accent, with a Hispanic twist, that Abby didn't recognize.

The wide brim of the woman's hat shadowed her face but from what Abby could tell she was beautiful; full red lips, high cheek bones and a rounded chin.

"Sure."

"Murallia," she offered, setting what looked like a Bloody Mary with a celery stick, cucumber wedge, and a couple shrimp around the brim on the table.

"Abby. What a beautiful evening, right?"

The woman plucked a shrimp off the edge of her drink. "It is. I'm renting a place and can't get over the sunsets and the color of the water. It's incredible." She popped the shrimp into her mouth.

Abby grabbed a fry and pulled, the cheese falling away, and stuffed it into her mouth. She continued eating. There was something about the woman that was *familiar* and begged her attention, yet she couldn't put her finger on it. She seemed young, yet old at the same time. A wisdom beyond her years. Abby's eyes wandered to the dropping sunset and the colors spreading over the water, then she searched the beach in hopes of spotting her dream man again.

Murallia placed a hand on Abby's arm. "It was a pleasure to meet you, and maybe we'll meet again soon."

He is here searching for you, accept and let him in. The dream man's face, chest, and their moments together smashed into the forefront of her mind.

Emerald Coast

The words coerced
themselves into her head,
invading her mind space.
She drew her arm back. It
wasn't that she had a
problem being touched in
a friendly way, or even
that the invasion wasn't
soothing, because for
whatever unknown
reason it gave her mind
purpose. No, it was the
act that someone
touching her could bring
about words, thoughts, or
was that part of her
extraordinary
imagination?

Chapter Seven

The moment with Murallia on the beach wouldn't go away. Her mind replayed all the strange things as she locked herself in her condo for the next few days, plunged heavily into her writing to free her mind of all the weirdness.

She did an internet search on all her symptoms; sudden craving for fresh meat, hallucinations, voices in her head, sudden sharp pains, and came up with nothing, forcing her to make a decision about her health and a doctor's appointment for a physical. She figured that was a good place to start.

Her dream man hadn't come around since she'd kept her sliding glass door locked tight. That was as encouraging as it was frustrating. Even imaginary sex was better than no sex. The line between fiction and reality was dim in her world.

After four days of locking herself at home

with no incidences she readied herself to leave. Slipping on a sundress and her usual flip flops she headed to the doctor's office, hoping for good news but ready to accept a referral to a psychiatrist.

The front desk was located in the middle of the large waiting room. After checking in she took the packet given to her and began answering the questions. The first page was basic; address, age, insurance, phone number. The next page asked about illness, diseases, and medications

she'd had or was on.
Never. She'd never been
sick, not even the
common cold or flu. She
never missed a day of
school as a child;
probably the only child in
history who had perfect
attendance, Kindergarten
through twelfth grade.
Like her parents always
said, the family had great
genes.

The last page asked
about family history and
of course there were no
issues, or none that she
knew of. Really, she didn't
know anything beyond
her grandparents. Maybe
there was some mental

illness factor that went way back, beyond them.

"Abigail Valaster," a nurse in seafoam green scrubs stood at the door, a clipboard in hand. She stood on the scale as the nurse took her weight and height. Then brought her to a room and checked her blood pressure and asked her to pee in a cup then return to the room and wait for the doctor.

Twenty minutes passed before the doctor entered the room. Her eyes on the paperwork as she flipped the chart. She glanced at Abby and smiled, pushing up the thin wrinkles on her round face. Round rimmed glasses over her eyes. "I'm Doctor Glasser."

Her smile disappeared and her eyes widened as she asked, "You've never been ill? You're not taking any medications?"

"Nope, never."

"You must have amazing genes," she replied with a chuckle.

"I guess. There's no history of any illness in my family. My parents say our genes are impeccable."

"It seems they're right. Your blood pressure is good. Your BMI is normal. It appears you are here for a physical and have had some recent discomfort in your spine?"

"Yeah, I went in for a massage and had to leave when he hit an area on my back. A radiating pain shot through my back, legs, and arms."

"Has it happened since?" the doctor asked, as she pressed on Abby's back.

Abby shrugged. "No."

"It's uncommon, but you have extra bones in your vertebra," said Dr. Glasser as she pressed on the area. Her voice calm like it was nothing, but to Abby it was like having extra genitalia.

Abigail cautiously responded, "What does that mean?"

"Probably nothing, for most people this would be operated on as an infant. Your spine seems remarkable and let's see you are…" Dr. Glasser riffled through the paperwork. "Here it is, and you're twenty-seven, it seems you have a birthday soon." She glanced up and met Abby's concerned gaze. "It's nothing for you to worry about; it's just the way you're made. Some people are born with tails, others with wings.

"Anything else going on?" the doctor asked.

At this moment Abigail felt like a freak and asked, "Wings, I have wings?"

The doctor responded assuredly, "Not exactly, just extra bones, the theory is ancient people may have had wings. Over time people lost them because we didn't need them. It's like wisdom teeth, some people have them and some don't."

Abigail, half joking and half serious, said, "You're telling me I'll never be able to fly?"

With a smile the doctor said, "I hate to disappoint you but, yes. Is there anything else you wanted to ask about?" she asked, leaning her back against the counter.

Abby sighed and was glad for patient doctor privilege and HIPPA laws. She twisted her mouth. "Yeah, I have been losing time recently, like a black out?"

A hint of concern lit Dr. Glasser's face. "Do you get headaches or dizziness?"

Abby didn't mention that she sucks blood and pulls out hearts during those blackouts. "No, I lose time and… sometimes have hallucinations."

"Tell me about those."

"I see things that aren't there, smells are more vibrant, and I hear things sometimes."

"Says here you are single, no kids. You are an author?"

"Currently I'm working on a novel. It's kind of crazy, about aliens. Historical fantasy." Her eyes became large and round to emphasize. "I'm currently starting a new spin-off series. It's a bit different. A prequel to my Surrender Time Saga."

"I have to confess; my son is addicted to your books. He's read them all at least twenty times. He'll be jealous I met you today but that's not why you're here." The next words from her mouth threw Abby for a loop. "Any chance you could be pregnant?"

She couldn't tell her about hot dream man and their rolls in the hay. It wasn't real anyways, was it? He hadn't shown up since she'd kept the door locked tight at night. It was in her head and worked like a placebo. She thought it worked, so it did. "I'm always very careful."

"When working on a novel in the past have you ever noticed anything odd about yourself?"

Abby thought for a second. "Yes… once, one

of my characters was a sleepwalker and I started sleepwalking, when I finished the novel I stopped."

"Increased senses, strange foods, black outs, it may all be related to stress from working too hard or not taking time for yourself."

She sounded like Julian. "My best friend says the same thing. He encourages me to set alarms and do daily things like chores, going out for dinner, exercise, and other things."

"Working from home is becoming more

common in this day and age. I encourage all my patients who work from home to set time aside for themselves. Schedule work time and *you* time."

Abby nodded. She was right, Julian was right, and she'd start setting schedules.

"I'm going to give you a pap smear to rule out anything female related. You would be surprised what can happen when a body's pH changes," she said in encouraging words.

Abby didn't feel this was the right time to tell her she'd never had a pap smear, much less ever set foot in a doctor's office, hospital, dentist office, or even had a vaccine, as she leaned back and put her feet in the stirrups.

A nurse came in as Dr. Glasser performed the pap. It was uncomfortable and not something she cared to do again but not the worst experience ever. When she finished, Abby sat up.

"The results from your pap smear and your lab work should be back in a week. I'll call and we'll set up an appointment then to review them. Before you leave, stop in next door and they'll get the blood work done for you."

Blood work?

As if Dr. Glasser saw the panic on Abby's face she said, "It's procedure and used to rule out any hormonal or other abnormalities. You've always been healthy. No need to worry."

Her words were comforting, but Abby's mind had a mind of its own. Maybe she'd contracted mad human disease, or a fungus was growing on her brain. She nodded.

Emerald Coast

The doctor left and Abby got dressed and stopped at the front desk, paid and got the doctor's blood order then walked next door. There were a few people already waiting, a mother with two small children, a young man in his early twenties and another man and woman who were young but seemed old. On the surface they couldn't have been more than her age but something about them underneath the skin made them much older, like Murallia.

She waited almost an hour before they called her back. They took so many vials of blood that she didn't think she had any blood left! The phlebotomist was nice. He joked with her while taking vial after vial and it wasn't such a bad experience, like the pap smear, but she was glad when it was over.

As she was leaving, the young but old couple was still waiting. It seemed they should have had their turn before her. She gave them a sorry expression and left.

Chapter Eight

She felt only slightly better, but now had other concerns. *Is it possible she was pregnant? Was her dream man real?* She decided he was, but was he really? *Would her blood work show some type of incurable disease?*

To ease her mind, she worked. Falling into her imaginary world was always a comfort and she had a deadline to meet. She also took the doctor's words seriously and set an alarm.

Jim became disturbed when his lovely daughter, recently out of college, met a young man. He wasn't exactly a young man. He was a shape-shifter with unique talents. He was able to speak telepathically. Jim couldn't understand everything he said but he knew he and his daughter conversed through their minds. It was a stream of consciousness that intersected with his. No shape-shifter he had ever met had been able to

communicate through
their mind.

He also sensed this
young man to be far older
than he appeared. He
could read the code inside
his cells and he was so
much more than he
appeared. The way of all
populations on Preavym
was to have a single mate
for life, one individual
that would forever hold
the heart of another.
There were no cheating,
affairs, marriages, those
were all human actions.
Humans did not mate for
life. Most humans jumped
from one partner to the
next and very few ever

found love. Humans were whores.

On Preavym, when soulmates found each other there was no stopping. They were each other's mushima. It was extraordinary and once they found each other there was no turning back. He could see his daughter loved this shape-shifter, but he couldn't understand why. They were not even the same species. It was programmed into the Zaras to stay away from shape shifters, elude them, and throw them off their game, not open their hearts to each other.

It was the same with shape-shifters. They hunted the Zaras, admired them and hated them all at once. He didn't always understand human nature and his daughter was half human, maybe it was that part of her that loved this man. She was uncharted territory.

He did not approve, but he couldn't keep her from him either. It was a part of her, designed into her being and he the same. They did not, by Earth standards, "get married". What they did was much more. Yes, he had married Rose because that is what humans did and she was human. His daughter and her man, Nos, developed a life together. They had a daughter and he and Rose adored her, but what was she?

She wasn't shape-shifter or Vampire or even human, but she was beautiful beyond words and very different than previously made Vampires who were all but destroyed for their lack of humanity.

Emerald Coast

On her twenty-eighth birthday she'd chose the immortal life, drinking Jim's blood. That was when she told him about Nos. He was immortal too and had come here from Preavym. Now Jim wasn't sure how a shape-shifter could become immortal, but it is what Nos' DNA had always told him.

With his daughter happily in love before the birth of their daughter, Jim continued his research on how to kill an immortal. No being could ever truly live forever, but an immortal couldn't be killed and that was the secret. An immortal could not be killed but they could end their own life.

The means for an immortal to die was the simplest, most fundamental element. It was also the element in his life that was hardest to control; it was part of his innate being, but if the desire were strong enough one could make it happen. He didn't know this for sure but was taking the chance. When his generation was designed there had to be a back door built for death.

Emerald Coast

His daughter was immortal and married another. Rose did not have many more years and he would go with her. There was no point to living on when he had found his one single life mate. It was a cruel trick his ancestors played on them and soon it would be his time to join them. The birth of Jim's granddaughter made him think: *She may also choose the immortal path or, since she was the hybrid of all hybrids, it may be chosen for her.*

Engrossed in her writing, her mind processing the words, she jumped when her alarm honked. She took a deep breath and turned it off. She was doing her best to stay on a schedule. To do what Julian and the doctor recommended. Maybe it was just stress and anxiety. Setting her computer on the charger, she entered her room and changed her clothes into something more presentable for public, pulled back her hair and slipped her feet into white flip flops.

She hadn't planned on stopping anywhere, just a long walk, maybe a sandwich from the food truck, but as she passed the Pirate's Cove she couldn't get past her inner voice that begged for a drink. She succumbed, using the excuse that it would do her good. It was a normal thing people did and she'd get plenty of exercise too, walking to and from pumping the endorphins.

There was an unusually small crowd which she blamed on the darkening sky. If it rained that meant she'd just have to drink another Zombie or maybe something lighter like a beer. Beer, yeah, that was a better choice. Her stomach moaned in complaint as the carbonated beverage settled into its emptiness. "Could I get a veg… a burger… rare?"

The bartender who had served her enough to know she was a vegetarian glared at her like she was an alien, one eyebrow raised. "A veggie burger, right?"

Abby sucked in her bottom lip, debating. She really wanted meat. She didn't understand that craving either but thought maybe her mojo was off since she was stressed or anxious or whatever. Or maybe it was her body's way of telling her that her diet lacked necessary nutrients. A veggie burger had plenty of protein and nutrients and she didn't want to alarm the bartender anymore as he stared at her like he didn't hear correctly. "Yes, please. Can I… get a couple slices of regular bacon on it?"

"Regular bacon, huh? You giving up the veggie thing?" His eyebrow still cocked as he wrote down her order.

"No, I just want to try bacon. Everyone talks about it so I thought maybe it wouldn't hurt," Abby said, shrugging her shoulders. "Besides, I don't think it really classifies as meat."

"You got that right." The bartender smiled and passed her order on to the chef.

Abby blew the air out her cheeks as rain began its descent. Tell-tale pitter patters hit the tin roof of the outside bar. Three guys, all seeming in their mid-twenties, splashed through the soggy sand as they ran toward the Pirate's Cove. Their feet clamoring on the wooden stairs as they entered the outside bar.

Two of the men were about the same height – tall – by Abby's standards, anyways. One was husky with a beard. The shorter man was more of a pretty boy with his fine features. The only other patron in the bar was an older man who was a regular. She'd never really spoken with him other than to say hello.

"I got this," one of the young men said, his voice gruff. She imagined he was the huskier one with the beard.

She stood corrected. When he got to the bar, she saw she'd pegged him wrong. He was the shorter one with a clean, pretty boy appearance. He glanced at her. She smiled and turned away, in no mood for small talk or being hit on.

He thought otherwise as he slid closer to her. "Looks like that beer is almost empty. I wouldn't want a pretty lady like you to go thirsty, can I buy you another?" he asked.

"Thanks, but no," she responded, taking out her phone to appear busy.

Why she was worried about being rude to this guy, she wasn't sure. She didn't get a good vibe from the group. It was like she felt their eyes on her, undressing her.

"I don't accept 'no'."

Really? That wasn't good! she thought. A man who doesn't accept no… He didn't mean anything harmful, she told herself. *Calm down!*

From the corner of her eye she watched him and listened as he ordered three beers and another of whatever the lady is drinking. The bartender glanced at her, as if asking approval. She made mouthed "no".

The young man leaned with his back against the bar. "You should join us."

She didn't respond. What was up with this guy? The bartender scooted the full beers towards the guy and placed one in front of Abby. The young man grabbed all three and left. She was relieved.

The bartender leaned over the counter. "Don't worry, that's on your tab." He pushed her burger in front of her and placed a ketchup and mustard on the bar top. Flipping the top bun over after a squirt of mustard, she took her first bite. The bacon was crispy and delicious! For a moment it took her mind off the group of men.

Normally Abby didn't have a problem with someone buying her a drink. But there was something about him – them – the group – as she continued eating her burger.

They laughed and poked fun at Gruffy. "Burn!"

"Brah. She's out of your league dude!"

"Shut the fuck up," he responded, taking a sip of his drink. She heard the slurp as if he was in her ear. She shook her head to get rid of the aggravating sound. Instead, words popped into her head. *I'll hit that tonight. Right over a table, doggy style. Bet that pussy's tight. Fuckable.* Voices in her head. She was cracking up! Julian's latest idea for a graphic novel plunged into her thoughts. *Am I psychic, telepathic?*

To make matters worse one of them lit a cigarette. The odor filled

her nostrils and an image
of black-spotted lungs
filled her brain and
purplish blood filled with
carbon dioxide and low
on oxygen pumped
through constricting
blood vessels. It turned
her stomach as she
swallowed a bite of
French fries.

If the rain wasn't a
down pour, she'd have
left, disgusted by the
young men. Some people
didn't have filters, but
their talk, words, not
really discussions, made
her nervous. She tried not
to hear or listen, focusing
on her email, the rain,

anything else, but their words were so loud and filtered through her ears.

She continued surfing her phone, ignoring them the best she could. Not hungry anymore, she slid her plate forward, asked for one more beer and paid her tab. As soon as the rain subsided, she was leaving.

She continued scanning her phone, attempting to ignore their vile language in her head. It was streaming without a shut-off valve. Heavy footfalls stopped at the bar beside her. From the corner of her eye, she spotted Beard.

"You should join us. We could use a female opinion," he stated as if she was a sheep that would follow his lead.

When she ignored him, he took that as an opportunity to continue talking, "Sorry about my friend, he has poor social skills." She saw the smirk on his face even though she wasn't looking. "I'm Trevor."

That was it! She swallowed the rest of her beer and scooted off the stool. Looking Trevor in the eye she seethed, "You and your friends are disgusting. Get your minds out of the gutter!" She stomped off into the rain that was starting to slacken.

She couldn't get far enough away from the young men as she ran. The soggy sand squishing between her toes. Flip flops in hand.

Some distance away she heard a female voice, "Keep it in your pants asshole!" Her words filled with tears and anger. Her heart thumping heavy in her chest. It grew louder, overtaking her voice, her words disappearing.

Emerald Coast

Abby closed her eyes, trying to push out the woman's conversation, instead it made the thumping louder. Blood coursed through the woman's veins, red with oxygen. Her lungs clean and pink. She didn't wonder how she knew, but was overcome with a desire. Within moments she was standing at the edge of the condo building. The woman sitting on her open patio with her head buried in her hands. Blood, clean and oxygenated, pumped through the woman's body. As if Abby's soul was abducted inside her own body. The woman's words grew distorted and Abby lost herself.

Nothing else in the world existed as pointed teeth erupted from Abby's gums, claws distended from her fingertips. She hurdled the short cement wall between them and grabbed the woman, pushing her long auburn hair to the side and sank her teeth into the warm flesh of her neck, blood pumping into her mouth and coating her throat as she swallowed.

Warm blood rolled down her chin, soaking her T-shirt. It was sweet and intoxicating. A life force. And she couldn't stop. The woman became limp in Abby's arms. She dropped her on the patio and wandered until she dropped into the sand twenty feet from her condo.

Chapter Nine

When she awoke, the sun was spilling over her from the sheer bedroom curtains. The succulent taste of blood on her tongue. Attacking the woman rushed into her brain, filling it up. It was as if something was inside her. Frantically, she touched her chin and pulled out her T-shirt. Nothing, no crusted blood, no red stain, but there was an odor. It was familiar, she just couldn't make it out — medicine. Her mind fuzzy. *How? Why was she imagining such horrific things?*

Gulping back her fear, she swallowed. *What had she done?* She had to find the woman, know if it was real or a nightmare. It seemed real enough but so did her horny rendezvous with the dream guy. She sprinted down the beach, her heels kicking up sand that beat against her legs.

After relentless searching, she found nothing. Raking her hands through her bedhead she dropped into the sand and lowered her head to her knees. It was like in the garage when she stripped the two men of their beating hearts, not a drop of blood or any remnant to give away the story. And, like the other incident, she fell asleep and woke up somewhere other than where she'd been.

What was happening?

Her back pocket buzzed. She didn't realize she'd had her phone. Taking it out of her pocket, a message from Julian blinked for her attention. Julian! He'd been gone much longer than usual. She wanted to tell him! She needed to tell someone! What would he say? Could she tell him she was going insane? Sign her into a loony bin.

The message read: *Home. TPC tonight?*

Yes! She needed him, even if she couldn't tell him everything. *Meet at my place.* She sent the message and he returned with a thumbs up.

She sauntered home, her mind replaying both scenes. She paced her condo as if on crack then opened her computer and searched her symptoms;

hallucinations, nightmares, losing time, bloodlust. After several 'vampires are real' articles, filled with garble from people who believed in them, some even making claims to be a vampire, she shut her computer down. She wasn't that crazy, not like the people who wrote the blogs.

In her Surrender Time Saga, Vampires were created. The ones humans fear, anyways. They are bloodlusting creatures that are easily killed with direct sunlight or a stake in the heart. They hate the smell of garlic and chives. The Zaras created them since they were sterile, then destroyed them because such creatures couldn't exist. They'd wipe out humanity and the Zaras loved life and humans.

She swung the door open, welcoming Julian with a huge hug. She needed the comfort. He folded his arms around her as she snuggled her face into his chest. The smell again. The same one as on her shirt. She still couldn't place it.

"I've only been gone a few days." Those few days to Abby were too many. Too many when she needed him. The visit with his agent was longer than usual.

She sniffed before pulling away. The odor nagging at her – peroxide! That wasn't important at the moment. She grabbed her purse off the back of a barstool. "Let's go."

He lifted an eyebrow. "What's wrong?"

He knew her well, too well. How much should she tell him? Maybe after a few zombies. She wasn't yet

ready to tell anyone she
was cracking up.
"Nothing, I'm glad to see
you." She shrugged and
pushed out the door,
making him take a step
backwards.

The walk to Pirate's
Cove was filled with small
talk. Abby decided to act
as normal as possible all
the while running the
scenario in her mind how
she would tell him about
the freakish things
happening to her. He'd
understand. After all, he
was her best friend. He
never judged and was
always open minded.

The sun was shining bright over the water, coloring it various shades of pink. She squinted her eyes, then dropped the sunglasses from the top of her head. She hadn't remembered a sunset quite so brilliant she couldn't look at it.

She swung for the first round of Zombies as Julian picked a seat at the wooden railing around the bar, facing the blinding sunset. She sucked a huge swallow of her Zombie and set his on the wooden rail.

"How's your story coming?" he asked,

swirling the plastic skull and crossbones stir in his drink.

She shrugged. A child ran past their spot and dove into the sand, catching a frisbee. "That must have hurt," she chuckled.

If he caught on that she was avoiding something he didn't show it as he sipped at his Zombie. "Like volleyball. Did I ever tell you that story?" He didn't wait for her response. "My dad was always after me to play sports. I create, not kick or throw around balls. Anyways, I tried out for the volleyball team. During tryouts, I served the ball and it ricocheted off the wall and hit the coach in the back of her head," he said between chuckles. "She dropped. Bam, hit the ground with a thud," he said using hand animation.

Abby's eyes grew wide. "You took out the coach?" She imagined her gym teacher in high school. How she hated that woman. Abby was never athletic either, something else she and Julian had in common. A giggle snuck up and rose to her throat, imagining her oversized PE teacher dropping like a rock.

"Gave her an egg-sized knot and a concussion." He grimaced, then put his hand over her head and pushed her down, smashing it into the wooden rail. A whoosh and breeze swept over her head moments before a clatter hit the wooden floor. "What the hell…" she mumbled. He let go and she rose, a questioning glare on her face.

Julian ignored her what-the-hell glare and stood then walked across the bar and picked up a green frisbee. He tossed it back to the kid, who smiled and ran off. *How?* He hadn't even been looking at the kid or the frisbee at but at her. Did he have eyes on the side of his head? She hadn't seen it coming from her peripheral. *How had he?*

Before sitting down, he ordered them another round of Zombies. This gave her time to contemplate more how he'd seen that coming. Once he sat, she asked, "How did you know?"

"I was watching. You weren't paying attention,

but it was coming straight at you."

She gave him the stink eye and corrected him. "You weren't watching. Your eyes were on me."

He gave her a quirky smile. "Thank you, Julian."

She twisted her lips, deciding to forget it and sucked away at her Zombie as they munched on an order of cheese fries with jalapenos.

By their third round of Zombies she was feeling good, really good, enough to start mindlessly talking. "People are enhanced. I think I'm enhanced. Listen, I see things that don't really happen and hear things that are happening like before I was too drunk, I smelled peroxide on you and the sunset was so bright it blinded me!" Her eyes grew large. "I went to the doctor and I have "proto wings"."

He mumbled something that sounded like *It's happening* under his breath. "What?"

He shook his head and shrugged. The breeze catching strands of his pink hair.

She paused and took another sip, holding up her hand when Julian opened his mouth to speak. "There's something wrong with me. I'm enhanced."

"Abbs." His face serious, eyebrows flat and eyes narrowed. "I have to tell you something." His fingers nervously tapped on the rail. Had he been as nervous as her? Was she so tied up in knots over her situation she hadn't noticed something was going on with Julian?

"I wasn't really with my agent all that time," he confessed. "I was somewhere else; you see…" He paused while Abby waited in anticipation. "Humans *are* more than they seem. Well, some are. Remember the Mayan People? They didn't really disappear overnight, but were transplanted north."

She stared at him, trying to see only one Julian, but at the moment she saw one and a half.

He continued when she didn't respond, "There were these creatures, werewolves, who sought to devour humans but the ancient gods helped them build

weapons and tools for
protection. All those
things science deems were
to help them see the stars
and what have you were
really tools for detecting
and protecting them from
wolves and other large
animals."

"Wolves, like errr,"
she growled.

"Yes. When it wasn't
enough the ancient gods
protected the people and
moved them further
north. Where do you
think Native Americans
came from? Anyways,
some humans have
evolved, becoming
enhanced if you will, and

have gained extra-sensory skills such as telekinesis, telepathy, precognition. You get the idea. Only humans keep it a big secret, besides the flakes on TV. Nobody believes that stuff, so our secret is safe."

"Your imagination is as vivid as mine." She chuckled. Through the cobwebs in her mind a hint of something flashed. He saw the frisbee...

"You see what I mean, even you don't believe. Believe this, I'm enhanced and the monsters are still out there."

Emerald Coast

She didn't want to accept what he was saying. If he was enhanced, what was she? Something more, her powers weren't good. They killed people. "You've been reading my books haven't you? Your brain has connected to mine. That's how we're enhanced."

"Of course, you're my favorite author, but this stuff is real. There's even top-secret military trained in killing the monsters."

Her mind caught up and her face lit up in understanding. "Wait!

You're a precog. That's how you knew the frisbee was going to hit me in the face!"

"That's why I'm telling you this."

"There's no way you saw that. I didn't even see it." She picked up her Zombie, unwilling to hear more, and staggered off the patio and into the sand. The several alcohols in the drink hitting her hard. Her mind reeling from the combination of alcohol and the bomb Julian just dropped on her.

Julian rose from his barstool. "Wait, Abby,"

he called after her,
stumble-walking in the
sand, drunk and trying to
catch up.

"Go away, Julian,"
she said, stomping
through the sand. She felt
betrayed. He saw the
future, if only seconds
ahead. He was something
more than human and she
probably was too. That
would make sense of all
the craziness. *Why wouldn't
he just tell her?* Because she
couldn't accept it herself.
A precog, she huffed. She
was something scary.
Something nightmares
were made of.

"Abbs," he touched her shoulder. "Stop, listen to me. The pyramids, sphinx, Stonehenge, all this was set up so long ago by the ancients as tools, technology to identify monsters in the sky. Eventually the monsters came and the tools and technology from the ancients detected them. The ancients taught humans how to fight the monsters and the whole planet was ready. They hunted the dragons to extinction, and werewolves and shifters until they became nothing more than lore." He raked

his hand through his hair.
"Why do you think all
those ancient civilizations
disappeared? They didn't
disappear at all, but killed
an alien species then
moved on. But what the
ancients never knew is
that, over generations,
humans evolved extra-
sensory skills, offensive
skills that keep them one
step ahead."

He said it as if to
convince her, to make it
okay that he kept it from
her. How long had he
known? Was his new
graphic novel even about
enhanced humans? *If any of*

it was even true, why tell the world now?

He continued, "The ancient gods aren't gods at all, but Vampires. They drink human blood and need us to survive."

Her face wrinkled into a cringe. Her eyes meeting his. "You see the future, you're evolved or enhanced or whatever and so am I… and your novel?" She put a hand over her mouth. She had some connection to a Vampire! Had one forced her to drink its blood then brainwashed her?

"I did see my agent, but I also am working on

developing my skills. The novel isn't real. It was my way of telling you what I am."

"You just did. Isn't this easier then lying?" Another thought hit her. His whispered-under-the-breath words, 'It's happening." It was easier to blame him, to be mad at him, than admit he made sense, because it might explain what was wrong with her. She could blame it on glamour.

"Abby, I didn't know how. Sorry." His eyes so remorseful, she couldn't be upset.

She grabbed his arms and shook with surprising strength. "What am I? Am I being stalked by a Vampire? Glamoured or whatever they call it?"

He swallowed. "I think you are a Vam…pire."

She sucked in a deep, deep breath. "Haaaa. A what? No, no. Don't accept it! I'm human. See?" She flailed her arms and danced in the tide. "Human," she sang, spinning in circles. A frenzy swirled inside her like a tornado. Vampire. No. No way! Anger bubbled to the surface

like hot lava. "Hell no!"
She stomped away.

"Abby, Abbs." She
didn't hear his feet behind
her as she stormed home.

Chapter Ten

Abby staggered into her condo, tossing her purse on the bar and collapsing onto the sofa. A cool breeze swept over her, tickling hair across her cheek. As her heavy eyelids dropped closed, a shadowy figure sitting on a chair on her balcony was the last thing she saw.

A finger traced up her arm, starting at the wrist and over her shoulder and neck. Warm, minty breath flooded her face.

"I had to see you," a masculine voice whispered in her ear. A finger circling her lips. His breath drawing nearer as his lips brushed hers.

She curled her arms around his neck and raked her fingers lightly through his thick waves. It was him, her dream man, meaning she was in dreamworld where he existed. Her lips met his with a fervent kiss. Desire burst through her in thick waves.

Her hand moved below his waist and felt his manhood. His hands moved below her shirt and kisses drifted over her breasts. His heavy breathing matching hers as their clothes became a pile on the floor.

"Where have you been?" she asked. His only response, heavy breaths on her face.

She pushed him upwards with unbelievable strength and forced him onto the couch as she straddled him. His fine features outlined by the light of

the moon streaming
through the open door.

She pushed herself
onto him and slowly
worked him into her.
Gently circling her hips.
His hands and lips all
over her as she posted her
hands against the back of
the couch and pushed
herself against him,
swallowing all of him.

Her body wracked
with convulsions of
pleasure with each
orgasm. The thump of
the couch hitting the wall
a quiet pounding in her
head. Their moans in
concert as she relaxed her
head against his shoulder.

His arms encircling her and holding tight as his juices exploded inside her.

Abby squinted her eyes against the brightness of the morning sun. The curtain around her sliding door blowing with the breeze. Pulling the blanket over her eyes she saw only him. The man who came to her in her dreams and vanished before the light.

The feel and scent of his body still fresh in her mind. She no longer cared if he was real. He felt real.

Emerald Coast

There was something she needed to remember. Something Julian had said, but their conversation was fuzzy at best.

After thirty minutes, she rose when her phone buzzed. The blanket dropping onto her lap, exposing her breasts. She stood and sauntered to the bar, then shuffled through her haphazardly thrown purse until she found her phone.

We're on the road see you in a few hours, love.

"Crap," she said out loud. "My parents!" She'd all but forgotten her birthday was tomorrow. Taking a sweeping glance over her condo, she needed to get to work. Her mom would be so upset to see her place such a mess.

After throwing on some clothes, she sprayed the surfaces with disinfectant cleaner and wiped them down. Her mom wouldn't be happy unless she smelled the bleach.

She scrubbed the toilet, the tub, and mopped the floors until her condo shined. She then lit a scented candle. Her hamper overflowed with clothes, so she grabbed an armload, losing something, and stuffed them into the washing machine. Going back for the something she dropped… it was the shirt she wore the night she sucked the blood of the woman on the beach. *Had that happened?*

The peroxide odor clung to it. She dropped it on top of the clothes and tossed a detergent pack into the machine when a red dot caught her eye. Bringing her face closer, she studied the spot. It was tiny, microscopic almost, but there. She closed her eyes and sniffed it. The sweet metallic scent jumped at her amidst the peroxide.

She rubbed spot remover on it and started the wash. On her phone she searched hydrogen peroxide and blood stains.

Hydrogen peroxide is an oxidizing agent… catalase present in blood… it's broken down into oxygen and hydrogen.

Blood. The words on the website were confirmation the day at the beach happened. Julian. There was something Julian said, something about her that validated what she felt in her gut. What she had been feeling. As much as she'd tried to deny everything happening to her, she couldn't anymore.

There was something going on and it was dangerous. If only she could remember… but all she remembered was how Julian pushed her head down as the frisbee whooshed over her and being upset at him. She couldn't even remember why.

Another text from her mom: *Be there in an hour. Can't wait to see you!*

"Mom. Why? This isn't the time!" she shouted. With everything happening to her, how would she explain any of it to her parents? Would she have to? Her parents always had a way of seeing through her as if they read her mind. A secret was impossible with them.

There was nothing she could do. They were on their way and wouldn't take no for an answer. They believed twenty-eight was a milestone birthday. She never understood it. Sweet sixteen, eighteen becoming a legal adult, twenty-one finally old enough to legally drink without a fake ID, even twenty-five car insurance was lowered, but twenty-eight? Her parents were eccentric.

She stripped her sloppy clothes off and tossed them onto the pile in her hamper and stepped into the shower. Adjusting the shower head, she set it to massage away her anxiety and stress.

Her condo clean, clothes clean, folded, and put away, and dressed in a springy sundress, she and her home were ready as she opened the door and let her parents in.

Chapter Eleven

bby's mother – Sabrina, her long golden hair tied back in a ponytail, with a sundress over her hourglass figure, the perfect MILF – folded her arms around Abby and squeezed. "I miss you!"

Her father – Zen, his thick, dark hair as always trimmed neatly above his ears – carried in their luggage. Muscles exploding from beneath his shirt. He dropped their luggage in the living room and pulled her into a bear hug. His thick arms molded around her and she felt safe. For that moment all her anxiety melted away and she wanted to cry into his expansive chest.

Her parents were eccentric, to say the least. Neither looked a day over thirty and they were always chipper.

"Is that steak I smell?" asked her mother as she followed her nose to the freezer.

Emerald Coast

Abby was taken off guard. She smelled the steak she'd bought and stuffed in the freezer over the bleach. Abby wasn't about to admit she'd bought it on a strange urge. She didn't think burdening her parents with her strange fugue episodes would solve anything. "I bought it for you and dad. I never have anything in the house for you to eat when you come."

"Thank you, sweetie," her father replied in his deep voice.

"We'll cook that tomorrow, tonight we're

dining out. We got reservations at that seafood place on the beach."

Abby knew the place. Every time her parents visited, they ate there. The food was good but Abby didn't eat any meat including marine life, although saliva bubbled in her mouth remembering those shrimp of Julian's she'd eaten.

It was a beautiful night for dining on the beach. The sunset was perfect for the lenses of a camera and a gentle breeze rolled off the coast, pushing Abby's hair to one side.

Her parents worked on devouring a lobster and crab legs, eating like food wouldn't be available tomorrow. Abby ordered a salad. She wanted to grab a crab leg but quelled that desire in front of her parents, avoiding the 'We told you one day you'd eat meat' lecture. No, she wasn't going down that road, at least, not yet.

"How's your book going?" her father asked after swallowing a large gulp of beer to wash down the crab leg he'd just devoured.

"Good. I'm about two-thirds done. I'll meet my deadline."

Sabrina brought her hand over and squeezed Abby's. "Have you found anyone special yet?"

There it was, the question. Last night's rendezvous with the mystery man came rushing back to her mind. He had to be real, had to be, but *how* she didn't understand. He'd appeared out of nowhere, never stayed, and disappeared into thin air.

"No." It was a safe answer.

"You should get out more, go to clubs, dancing. Not stay cooped up in your condo," Sabrina said, concern in her eyes.

"I live in the small, one-horse beach town of Nirvana, Florida. There are no clubs, just a couple of bars." Her blood started to boil thinking about the disgusting men who hit on her at the Pirate's Cove a few nights ago. "Besides, you wouldn't want me dating the trash around here, not if you knew what they were like."

Zen's eyes narrowed. "Your mother and I both want what's best for you and we hate seeing you go through life alone. A life partner is such a blessing when you find your mushimo."

What? Did he just say… mushimo? He must be reading her books. That wouldn't be a surprise. Her parents were always overly involved. When she was in girl scouts her mother went on every camping trip. Dance lessons: they stayed for every lesson and every recital. When she wrote the award-winning short story at twelve it was them who made it go viral. She had them to blame for her success. Weighing the pros and cons, they were most definitely helicopter parents at the same time they loved her with all their hearts. "I know. There isn't any dating material around here. Julian and I get together a couple times a week. Even he's disappointed in the limited selection."

Abby turned the conversation to their lives and they spent the rest of dinner catching up. No more questions about her private life. She gave them her room to sleep in and took the couch. She was glad she'd remembered to change and wash the sheets.

The next morning, she awoke to the smell of coffee, which she didn't drink, and steak and eggs. Dad brought the steak out. She chuckled inwardly. He loved to cook and did so more than her mother.

"Here, baby," Sabrina said as she set a cup of steaming green tea on the bar. "Happy

Birthday!" She kissed the top of Abby's bedhead.

"Thanks, Mom."

Her father slid the extremely rare steak onto a large plate and cut it into halves. Abby watched, her mouth salivating at the sight and smell. Red juices spilling onto the plate. "Did you want to try a bite?" he asked.

She fought the urge to grab the steak and stuff it into her mouth with her hands. "No, thank you."

Her father pushed a plate of scrambled egg substitute and jellied toast in front of her while he handed Sabrina of a half a very rare steak, runny eggs mingling with the red juices of the meat.

"We should go for a walk on the beach. Mother, daughter time. I've missed you," Sabrina suggested.

By the look in her mother's eyes she knew it was something she had to do. It wasn't that she wasn't lucky to have the parents she did but, at twenty-eight, they didn't need to hover over her anymore. She nodded.

After breakfast, Zen nearly pushed them out

the door, insisting that he'd clean the kitchen.

What was so important her mother needed to say? Abby wondered as they strolled the beach to a secluded nook only locals knew about. They sat on a rock overlooking the tiny tide pool filled with baby fish.

Her mother, usually cheery and easy-going, wrapped Abby's hands in hers, her eyes filled with sincerity and concern. Abby knew the look. It was the same one she gave her the time Abby skipped school with her best friend, taking the bus into the city. It meant: "Don't say a word, just listen."

With her mouth clammed and her ears fully opened, she listened as her mother began. "Abby, this day has been decided since you were conceived. I know over the last few months your body and mind have been going through a series of changes."

Abby's mind didn't quite register her mother's words. "These changes can't be explained under any human terms. I went through similar changes when I was your age but your father was there to assist me through them just as I will assist you. My father took me aside and explained everything much as I am about to do with you. We are not like everyone else, but we are not alone either."

Abby's brain finally began processing her mother's words. *Changes… my father… I will assist you…* How could her mother even possibly know all the weird stuff happening to her recently? *Did it happen to her too?* Taking the defense, Abby said in a huff, "What are you talking about, Mom? Life is fine. It's normal."

Her mother gave her the eye and Abby shrugged. Loosening her hands from her mother's grip she placed them in her lap.

"You are, we are, special, Abby. My father, Jim, was from the planet Preavym. He was a Vampire and my mother, Rose, was completely human."

No way! Those were the characters in Abby's book. There's no possible way her mother knew that. It was impossible! That would make her mom Sabia and her father Nos but those weren't their names. Abby interrupted, "You're telling me you are half-Vampire?" So being a nut was in her family. "There's no such THING!"

Her mother's eyes widened and her eyebrows shot up into Vs. Her voice carried a firm, 'shut up and listen' tone. "I am half human and half Vampire. Your father is not human at all and his birth name is Xenos. He was born long before his species knew humans existed. He was born on

Preavym, his father a dragon and his mother something unique. She was a ground Fira with Zaras characteristics. You are something different, not born of a test tube but the natural process of two hybrids mating. You shouldn't be possible, but yet you are! You are the most splendid, powerful creature on this planet!"

No, no, no, and absolutely no! Her mother couldn't know any of this. They were sharing the same delusion! It was her story. "Hell, fucking no!" Abby shouted as she jumped to her feet and

ran off. Tears pouring
from her eyes. There was
something Julian said the
other night that was
slowly rising in her
subconscious.

Chapter Twelve

bby kept running. Not paying attention to where she was going, she ended up in front of Julian's home. His words from the other night replaying in her head, '*You are a Vampire… You are a Vampire.*' They couldn't all be sharing the same delusion, could they?

She swallowed hard and walked up the concrete path to his front door. She knocked and waited but there was no response. After a few minutes she turned and stepped away, heading down the walkway towards the road when she heard the door open.

"Abby," Julian's voice filled her ears. "Happy Birthday!"

She turned to look at him. He wasn't alone, she smelled someone else too. "About last night. I'm sorry, Jules." She wanted to say more but alone, behind closed doors.

"Abby, I would have reacted the same way. I shouldn't have dumped it on you. I'm sorry." He stepped out of the house in his bare feet. A tall male figure walked to the door behind him.

She sucked up her sniffles and wiped her eyes, then painted on a faux smile. "You have company. I'm gonna go."

He walked closer. "Abby, you are my best friend and we need to talk."

She shook her head. "We will. I have to go, you have company." She figured the man in the doorway was his latest partner or someone he was at least beginning to see. He hadn't said anything last night so the man must be very new.

She sprinted away before he could say anything more or attempt a hug. Tears fell again, draining from her eyes like a faucet without a shut off valve. Her legs carried her towards the bridge connecting the mainland to the tiny island. The sun beating hard against her head and blinding her eyes.

All she saw was white and spots when she blinked. She panicked and stopped. Groping with her hands, she felt for the rail on the bridge then sucked in a deep breath and squeezed her eyes shut. The sounds of traffic, animals, people on bikes, and walkers formed a sort of echolocation as she slowed her pace, allowing the noises to guide her.

At her condo building, she rushed into the dark garage, choosing not to use the front door. Her face a teary, snotty mess she didn't want people to see her even if her eyes wouldn't allow her to see them. The darkness of the garage brought her vision back.

Emerald Coast

Through the tears she
made out the parked cars,
cement barriers, and
elevator. *What the hell was
happening to her?*

*Were they right? Was
she a… a… a… Vampire?*
She didn't want to think
about it, but it made
sense. As she walked past
the area where she pulled
the beating hearts out of
the two men, she
envisioned it again as if it
was happening over and
over. Her thoughts
brought back the woman
on the beach and how she
attacked her, sinking
fanged teeth into her
neck.

Her senses had been more acute and her mother knew things, things she couldn't know unless they happened to her. It made sense in a demented way. But if her mom was only half human and her dad a ground Fira or shifter, flying Fira or dragon and Vampire. *What on Earth would that make her? She was a freak!* That's what she was. A hybrid born from the union of two hybrids, as her mother suggested.

The soothing music in the elevator did little to ease her tension as she worked up the nerve to confront her mom – her parents. They always worked as a team.

The elevator door opened, and she exited, stopping short of the door that would carry her back outside and the glaring sun. *How did she forget sunglasses?* Her eyes had always been sensitive to the sun. What was happening now was far and above anything she'd ever experienced, yet she knew never to go outside without a pair of sunglasses.

Squeezing her eyes closed, she pushed the door open. The warmth of the sun beamed on her head, she felt its light through her eyelids, and it stung. She covered them with her hand as she let the sounds of her own footsteps guide her towards her condo.

Once outside the door, she took one last deep breath before turning the knob. Once inside she slammed the door shut and opened her eyes slowly. "Close it!" she yelled as light streamed from the open sliding glass door.

Footsteps pattered towards the door. By the sound, she knew they were her mom's. Heftier footsteps came towards her and a large arm wrapped around her back and guided her towards the couch. She snuggled into her dad. Tears streaming down her face.

"What's happening?! What the fuck is happening?" she sniveled.

The couch cushion on the other side dropped as her mom sat down. "Abby, I know. I went through all this too. I'm sorry we didn't warn you. I'm so sorry, baby."

Twenty-eight. The age Sabia was to claim her Vampire legacy. The age

Jim said the granddaughter needed to be. She was twenty-eight. Jim warned the child might not have the choice. *She may not have a choice.* Through choked sobs, Abby asked, "What the hell am I?"

"You are a powerful creature, more so than any other alive," her father said as he gently rubbed her arm.

"We always hid you out in the open. Your Vampire energy took the place of your grandfather's, who welcomed death the day you were born. He designed me and the choice to accept what I am and become it; an immortal or to choose humanity. This is the most special and life changing moment you will ever experience. You now have a choice to make and only you can make it." Her mother's words stated in a gentle soothing tone as if this was natural or normal.

"I don't know. If I don't become like you, will I always have these cravings and strange experiences? Will I eat raw meat and drink human blood?" *She may not have a choice… She may not have a choice…* Jim's words echoed relentlessly in her mind.

"The decision you make will not take away your humanity, which you fear losing. It will accentuate your humanity and help you control the desires you fear. You must drink my blood just as I did my father's." Abigail's mother – Sabrina or was it Sabia? – extended her claws and held one vertical to her vein.

Abby sucked in a few deep breaths and nodded, then wiped the tears from her face. It was all too much at one time. She stared at her mother's arm. *Did she want to be immortal?* She did want control over her urges. "What about the men in the parking garage and the woman on the beach?"

Her father cleared his throat. "You are powerful and there are those who want you deceased. Two of them were the men in the garage. The woman on the beach, you didn't kill. She was saved in time. By taking your mother's blood you will have control over those urges."

"What happened to the bodies?"

"They were cleaned up," her mother stated.

"Vampires?"

Sabrina nodded. "They've been watching you and taking care of situations."

A thought struck Abby. "Mom, I have wings! Oh my god. Some people are born that way. There are others with Vampire blood that don't know. Vampires are born that way and my blood... They took my blood!"

Emerald Coast

"It's okay, honey, the vials were retrieved and destroyed and yes you have wings, but they may be different than mine. You are also dragon like your father. And, yes, there may be people with small amounts," she sucked in a breath, "of Vampire in them."

Abby chuckled, remembering the vision where she was flying, and her dream man was swimming beneath her as a shark. "I can fly!" She stood and paced the living room while her parents waited expectantly on the couch.

She discussed her choices with the angels on her shoulders. *If I take the blood, I will be a powerful being and possess great strength and be something nobody else is — a freak of nature. But a powerful one. I would also be immortal, which means I won't age or die. If I don't, the strange things will keep happening and people will keep coming after me. I won't be singly a Vampire but can't singly be a dragon or a shifter or a human. It would be safer, and I'd be able to defend myself better if I accepted Mom's blood.*

Abby walked to her mother and sat cross-legged on the ground. She made the decision. Taking her mother's wrist, she lifted it to her mouth. Her mother sliced it vertically with a claw-like nail that transformed in front of her eyes. She pressed her mouth against her mother's wrist and let the blood flow over her tongue and down her throat.

It was tangy and sweet. She sucked harder with desire. Her whole body tingled with sensations and every beat of her and her mother's hearts throbbed inside her head until they became one.

Her mother pulled her arm away. "Do you feel it?"

Abby felt as though she was floating in a fuzzy warm place and suddenly a bolt ran through every artery and vein in her body, exploding in her heart. Her already acute senses had just tripled in one instant and she could feel a wave of energy flowing in a continuum within her body.

Sabrina smiled as she watched her daughter reflecting in her mind how she had felt that day when she drank her father's blood.

Abby fell backwards, relaxing against the floor. The ceiling fan above her whooshed in slow motion. Sounds slowed and voices stretched, odors of all sorts assaulted her nostrils.

Her mother lay back on the floor next to her and took her hand. "It will pass when the blood has pumped efficiently through your system, but I will have to teach you to control your senses."

A knock at the door brought Abby back as she lifted upwards.

Chapter Thirteen

Her father stood and walked to the door, a wide smile on his face. She glanced at her mother who wore the same smile.

Whatever was on the other side of the door made her heart pump out of her chest. Peppermint and fabric softener, and something else.

Zen opened the door. Abby didn't need to

Emerald Coast

look to know her dream
man was on the other
side. She didn't care how
her parents knew as she
bolted off the ground and
to the door, stopping
short when she soaked in
his presence.

His eyes took her in
as he stepped forward.
She moved with him and
allowed his arms around
her waist as she guided
him towards the bedroom
and closed the door.
There were many things
to say but not until after
she'd had her fill.

He lifted her up
while she straddled his
legs and brought her

mouth to his in a long kiss. Their tongues hungry, and their bodies hungrier. He lowered her onto the bed, and they stripped away each other's clothes, tossing them. His mouth and tongue followed her curves as she moaned, raking her fingers across his back.

They tangled in the sheets and she pushed him over, straddling him, when wings erupted from her back. "Holy shit!"

He chuckled. "Put those away."

"I don't know how." Really, she didn't. She

didn't even know how they came out.

"They're beautiful, like shiny white leather leave them out," he said breathlessly between kisses.

Their bodies pressed against each other, moving in pleasure. She didn't even notice her wings drop on their own.

After they had their fill, she lay in the crook of his arm. "What is your name, mystery man?"

"Juanito. And you, mystery woman?"

"Abby."

How could she be upset? Yet part of her was. "Did

you…" she couldn't find a way to say the words.

"You weren't ready yet," he said as if reading her mind.

"How… How would you know that?" She sat up, glaring at him.

"I grew up in a world you are only beginning to see."

"So you thought it was okay to sneak inside my home or invade my thoughts?"

He smiled. "I didn't invade, but was invited."

She huffed, leaning back against the pillow.

His finger traced her leg. "I've always known

what I was. My mother Murallia, she taught me since I was a baby. My father was a shifter of some sort. I never met him and so I had no one to teach me the *shift*. It was your father who helped me and now we will teach you."

Abby's eyes narrowed. "You know my father?" She was more surprised at that than hearing his mother was the woman she met at the beach while eating cheese fries.

"Yes, your father. He is a shifter but, like me, is also Zaras. An experiment on his mother Etiari maybe. She always knew she was more than what she seemed and he too."

When she thought her mind was done being boggled, he scrambled it all up like eggs. With the revelation, it was Julian who came to mind. *Why now? Why if all this really exists did he confide humans' abilities in her?* Because she was a… a… quadbrid. A monster of all monsters. No. Not Julian. It was something far more subtle and they'd discuss it privately. Not until she knew more would she confide his secret.

Emerald Coast

Juanito's fingers traveled over her naked abdomen as he kissed where his finger touched. "We are special, Abby. We shouldn't exist, but we do."

Upset, she didn't give in right away to his taunting and touch that spread warm tingles throughout her body. Unable to resist him for long, she wrapped her hands around his head and lifted it from her belly. She pressed her lips against his and locked in a kiss. She slid beneath him.

Esma Rose

Chapter 1

sma stood at the crosswalk. The light on the other side flashing red. Her eyes fixed on the light until it blurred. She wrestled with her thoughts. *Was she too hard on him?* She and her boyfriend got into a fight. Esma left and now, moments later, stood in front of the red hand light, staring at it.

When they fought it was always petty. *Was she petty and a vain vixen?* He called her one and it angered her. She was a one man at a time gal and it was important for a woman to maintain her youth and always look presentable.

The street lights glowed above her, shining onto her plaited auburn hair hanging beneath her white hat. She wore a long white leather coat matching her hat and knee-high mahogany boots. The chilly air flushed her cheeks and nose but she didn't notice the cold.

Cars beeped and honked as they zoomed past while she stood staring at the light. Snowflakes fell softly, dropping onto her and the ground.

"Are you okay?"

She zoomed out of her thoughts and glanced at the man next to her. The muscles beneath his shirt defined enough to see their outline through the loose-fitting button-up shirt he wore. His slacks, made of lightweight material, were crisp and ironed.

His face edged with a strong jawline and his lips full, but not too full. A well-manicured mustache beneath his straight nose. Sandy brown hair streaked with gray covered his head and was neatly trimmed above his ears. But his eyes were his most striking feature. They were a piercing brown that smiled warmly at her.

"I will be," she responded.

He pressed the walk button and the blinking red hand changed to a solid white person. They crossed the street.

"You stood in front of that light several minutes. Are you sure everything is fine?"

She adored gentlemen and thought again of her boyfriend and their silly arguments. A smile tugged at the corners of her lips. "I got into a little disagreement with a friend and now I'm overthinking it."

"You can never overthink a problem with a friend and it's never too late to make everything right again," he stated, walking in stride with her.

"This time it is," she answered with a hint of sorrow.

"How's that?"

Esma ignored his question. "This is my house. Thank you, uh… I never got your name," she said, brushing a white gloved hand along his.

"Gracen Halinger. A beautiful lady should never walk home alone." He smiled and watched as she walked up the stairs to her house.

She strolled inside and flicked on the light,

setting her keys on the small table beside the doorway. She peeled off her coat, gloves, and hat, hanging them in the closet, then shifted and cautiously stepped into the living room. Her boyfriend lay on the couch, his eyes closed and chest still. She leaned close to him and didn't feel his breath. "Honey." She gently shook his shoulder. His arm dropped off the side of the couch, touching her abdomen.

Registering he was dead, she screamed!

Chapter 2

The gentleman didn't hesitate upon hearing her scream and ran up the steps to her home, taking them two at a time with his long stride. He burst through the door, following her screams. She was kneeling on the floor, her brown eyes huge and tears falling across her cheeks. Laid out on the couch was an olive-skinned man with dark coffee hair and a neatly trimmed matching mustache.

He rushed towards her, eying the man. "Is he--."

She cut him off with a whimper, "Yes."

"Call 911," he demanded as he grabbed a poker from the fireplace and stalked the house. The living room led back to the hallway. It was long. Across from him was a dining room. A bouquet of roses in the center of the table set inside a crystal vase. The room was empty and led into a kitchen. The square room contained a breakfast nook and island, pots and pans hung

above. All still and clear,
he went back into the
hallway, peeking into the
living room. Still squatted,
she was on the phone.

He sighed, assuming
she was on the phone
with a 911 operator. The
rest of the house
contained two bedrooms,
a hallway bath and master
bath with a large garden
tub. Candles were placed
around it and their scents
lingered in the air even
though not lit. He cleared
each of the rooms and
closets. Convinced no
one else was in the house,
he returned to her.

Sirens blaring told him she'd called and they would be in the home within minutes. "The house is clear," he said as he placed the fire poker back in its place.

"Thank you," she managed with a shaky voice.

She stood in a royal blue dress that hugged every soft feminine curve of her body. The color brought out the red in her hair and the deep russet in her eyes. She was a beautiful woman, more so than any woman he'd laid eyes on. His urge was to take her in his arms and sweep her into his embrace. He suppressed the urge and grabbed her supple hand, caressing it in his. She gazed into his eyes.

The policeman rang the doorbell and hollered in a firm voice, "Ms. Rose."

"Come in, please," she responded, dropping his hand and entering the hallway.

The policeman introduced himself as John Neelmeger. He wasn't taller than five foot six, with a bell-shape. His small eyes set inside a face of dough and thick salt and pepper hair greased back but not enough to cover the natural wave. He took Esma and Gracen aside as his partner checked the house and the paramedics confirmed the body was DOA.

Gracen didn't leave, but answered all the questions and listened while she responded to their inquiries. It was her boyfriend lying dead on the couch. There were no signs of forced entry and no marks or blood, nothing that gave any clues to how he died. After the autopsy they'd have a better clue what killed him, but they were assuming nature took its course early for him as he wasn't more than thirty.

Only an hour earlier they'd gotten into an argument and she left on a walk. That's when Gracen found her staring at the light, snowflakes diving from the sky and puddling around her boots. His heart leaped from his chest when he spotted her.

Her oval face and red pouty lips made it impossible for him not to reach out to her. "You can't stay here. Let me take you to a hotel."

Her russet eyes shifted, meeting his. "Thank you. Let me grab my coat."

He nodded and held her coat as she slipped her arms inside the sleeves and gracefully tugged her gloves over her hands and placed her hat on at an angle that drove him wild. He didn't place her over twenty-five, while he appeared at least fifteen years her senior.

The snow now inches high and still falling would make the

walk uncomfortable, so
Gracen hailed a cab and
the two squeezed into the
back seat. She sat like a
lady with her back straight
against the seat and her
hands folded in her lap.

"Stop at the Royale
please," said Gracen to
the driver. He turned and
met her eyes. "Allow me
to cover the cost."

"You've done so
much already. I don't
think I would have made
it through everything
without you there," she
said in a demure voice.

He smiled. "It's my
pleasure and I won't have
it any other way. A lady

such as yourself shouldn't have to face such drama alone. I will check on you in the morning." He grabbed her hand and squeezed.

"Thank you, Mr. Halinger." She squeezed his hand in return and stepped out of the cab.

He watched as she entered the hotel and called the front desk, making sure she got the best room and putting her stay on his credit card.

He lay in bed that night unable to take his mind off her. Her eyes such a unique shade of brown, almost red mixed

with her dark auburn hair,
long legs and perfectly
proportioned body she
was a dream. His mind
finally shut down enough
for sleep to come but she
didn't leave his thoughts.

Her soft hand took
his and they walked
backwards to the bed,
their mouths met in a
passionate kiss. Once they
reached it she broke her
lips away from his and
unbuttoned his shirt, one
by one, exposing his
chest. She ran her fingers
through the thin patch of
wiry hair covering it,
bringing her lips close she
dropped kisses on it

making a straight line
leading to his belt.

An intense desire for
her raged inside him.
He'd never wanted a
woman so much and felt
an urgency to thrust
inside her but as a
gentleman he waited,
brushing his hands over
the back of her hair as she
unbuckled his belt and
worked the button and
his zipper, letting his
pants drop to the floor.
He tilted his head back,
his eyes staring sightless
at the smooth cream
ceiling as she engulfed his
penis with her moistened
lips

Emerald Coast

Tenderly, he pushed
her backwards onto the
crimson satin duvet,
lifting her cobalt gown
over her luscious legs,
displaying her nub and
revealing a neatly trimmed
patch of sleek dark
auburn hair. He wanted
nothing more than to
please her as he brought
his mouth to her clit and
wiggled his tongue over it,
sliding it in circles around
the lips then driving it
into her vagina. It was
syrupy sweet like sucking
on a cherry lollipop. Small
moans of pleasure
escaped her lips as her

body jolted with the pleasure he brought her.

"I want you," she whispered, so quietly he barely heard it.

He guided his tongue across her belly and chest as he scooted forward on the bed until his hands rested beside her shoulders and his mouth met hers. He rested the tip of his cock at her moistened entrance and brushed lightly. Her hips met his movements, driving him over the edge. He fought his craving to plunge inside her. Building the desire, he inched inside her until her tight vagina swallowed him. The walls crushing against his cock as their bodies met in waves of pleasure, whimpers and moans breaking the silence in the air.

A sudden crash awoke him. Bolting upright, his sensuous dream faded but his dick throbbing and hard as a steel blade reminded him. Juices glistened from the tip to his groin. He swiped the liquid and brought it to his nose, inhaling in her scent, causing the blood in his body to pulse and rush further into his already swelling, hardened cock. Unconcerned and clueless how her juices left his dream, he brought his finger to his mouth and sucked her syrupy juices off it. He breathed heavy and crashed back onto his pillow. Wrapping his hand around his cock, he moved it quickly up and down to relieve the pressure building in his genitals. Cum squirted from the tip as another crash blasted his ears.

Chapter 3

fficer Neelmeger sat at his desk cleaning up paperwork before going home. The last call, and lovely Ms. Rose, embedded in his thoughts. There was something about her besides her obvious beauty. It was something that attracted him so much he wanted to strip off her clothes and do her against the wall in her house at the crime scene, but it also scared him.

His cop sense told him something was askew but the evidence pointed at the man dying of natural causes. There was no forced entry, nothing was stolen from the house according to Ms. Rose, and he bore no struggle marks or blood. The young man simply died. He forced the case to the back of his mind as he wouldn't know anything until the autopsy came back.

No matter how hard he tried, her face continued to stay at the front of his mind. He settled into bed, wrapping

an arm around his wife
and quickly fell into sleep.
A dark shadow moved
over him and drifted
towards his chest.
Suddenly breathless, he
coughed and his eyes
popped open. The
shadow slunk to the
ground. He lifted himself
out of bed and wandered
to the bathroom, pouring
a Dixie cup full of water.

The dark shadow
moved behind him. He
turned quickly and the
shadow formed into the
shape of a man. He
watched with wide eyes as
its face gained color and
shifted into the dead man

from his call. It reached out a tendrilled appendage and wrapped it around his arm. He struggled against it but the tendril became a solid hand holding him in a tight grip.

His gun was in the drawer beside the bed and he doubted it would do much damage against the half-man, half-shadow creature. His pulse quickened. The man's mouth moved but no sound came out. Its grip constricted on his arm and another tendrilled appendage grabbed his other arm and, becoming solid, squeezed him tightly. His legs free, he kicked at a shadowy leg but his foot went straight through.

"What are you?" he demanded, his pulse rushing through his body like a waterfall. He had the sudden urge to pee.

The creature's mouth moved again, but still no sound, and its brown eyes burned into his.

"Honey. John!" said the familiar voice of his wife along with the familiar shoulder shake. The one she usually reserved for the nights he snored.

He opened his eyes and blinked at her face. Short blond hair circled her round face and round blue eyes stared at him. It had only been a dream, he sighed with relief. "Was I snoring?"

"No, you were wrestling and nearly knocked me off the bed," she stated in a shaky voice.

He shrugged and raked a hand through his hair. "Long night. Let's go back to sleep."

She lay down, curling onto her side. He rested himself against her and wrapped an arm around her but didn't go back to sleep right away. He narrowed his eyes and stared at his arm. Enough moonlight illuminated it that he distinctly saw a bruise forming in the shape of a hand.